I ASKED THE MOON

PAUL A. RAYES

ANORI PRESS LC

I ASKED THE MOON

PAUL A. RAYES

I ASKED THE MOON

Publisher's note: This is a work of fiction. Names, characters, places, and incidents either are the product of the author's imagination or are used fictitiously. Any resemblance to actual events, locales, or persons, living or dead, is entirely coincidental.

ISBN: 979-8-9863494-0-4 (Paperback) / 979-8-9863494-1-1 (Hardback) / 979-8-9863494-2-8 (Ebook)

Library of Congress Control Number: 2022910992

Edited by Kristen Corrects, Inc.

Cover art design by Robin Locke Monda

First edition published 2022

AUTHOR WEBSITE

Scan code below to access the book playlist, and to connect with the author.

www.itspaularayes.com

1

———

THE DREADED REUNION

D o you remember your first crush? Or the first time you really wanted someone to be your friend?

I sit in my car facing the lakeside restaurant, listening to Indochine's "2033," staring through the windshield at the faint glow of the moon on this hot summer evening. "What am I doing here?"

I hated high school. Yet here I am, at our ten-year reunion. Thinking about times past and all the people I used to know makes my hands sweat and my eyes itch. It makes me think back on a period in my life when I wanted time to stop. When I wanted the world to pause so I could breathe. Have you ever felt like that?

His name runs through my mind again. A name that has lingered in the back of my head for all eternity. My eternity, at least.

I text my childhood best friend before pulling the keys out of the ignition. *Going in. See you inside.*

She immediately replies. *K.*

K? I look down at the screen, brows furrowed. I think too

I

much about context and clarity. When replying to text messages, I use *alrighty* instead of *K*. That one-letter response just gives me mixed signals. I might think you're angry with me or something. Am I crazy?

As I walk through the parking lot of the restaurant, I'm reminded of the days where I walked through the lot to the side of the school entrance. I used to be able to pick out the cars that belonged to my friends and acquaintances: Dana and her nearly new Escape, Kayla and her dad's always new BMW, Samantha with her old Ford Focus—a car many people in my school drove. It's a different story here today in front of this restaurant. I can't tell who owns what. Most of these people have been blank from my mind for the last decade.

I enter the private room to the right of the restaurant entrance and am signaled by a small group of girls huddled over a table close to the bar. Should I have said women? We're in our late twenties now. Funny, isn't it? I still don't see myself as an adult. Whenever I think of people my age, I think of them as girls and boys. Anyway, I instantly recognize them, a few former school friends who sat with me during lunch almost every day.

A sinking feeling seizes my stomach as regret falls over me. I ditched everyone after graduation. High school made me feel trapped, and in order for me to free myself, I had to create a new life without all of them. I could have tried to keep in touch. Instead, I did nothing. These girls treated me kindly at school, something I needed then. I know everything about them and their adult lives now thanks to social media. And yet here I am, a stranger reemerging from the shadows after a decade of silence.

"Hey! It's been too long. How've you been?" asks Kayla, looking for something in the purse hanging from Samantha's seat, her hair still strawberry blonde and wavy like I remembered.

"Yeah. We haven't seen you since the bonfire at Michelle's house the weekend after graduation," Samantha says, pointing to Michelle, who's pulling back her dark curls.

"It's been a long time. Hey, have any of you been in touch with Dana?" I nervously ask, gesturing to the empty chair across the table.

"No," replies Nicole, sipping on something like a vodka cranberry.

Who still drinks those?

"She told me she wasn't coming." Kayla pulls an e-reader from the hanging purse.

The table looks at me in confusion. Am I ruining a surprise for them? A feeling of uncertainty falls over me as I realize that Dana could be ditching me. *Dana wouldn't do that again though*, I think. *At least I don't think she would.*

The senior class vice president approaches the podium at the end of the room; the class president no longer lives in the country from what I gathered after stalking her on Facebook. The VP begins recounting times past, and a knot in the pit of my stomach starts to form. So instead of taking a seat, I walk over to the bar. I need a drink if we're going to talk about those days. I don't understand how people speak of the past in fondness. The past is the past, leave it there. Then again, I did show up. There must be a reason, though truth be told, I couldn't have named it.

Have a good time honey. Send me pictures of your friends, my mom texts as I'm about to order a drink. I roll my eyes.

I stand, annoyed, at the bar with a Canadian rye whisky in hand since the wine selection is overpriced. I would have paid more for the ticket if it were open bar.

Looking across at the top of the room where the podium stands, our class vice president still speaking, I notice the entrance door slowly closing. *Dana?* I straighten my back, eyes wide open dissecting the room trying to find the new face. I make awkward eye contact with several of my ex-classmates, but there's no one new in sight.

I tip the bartender after shooting the drink in my hand, then order another. Trust me, you'd also want another.

"Hey. Give me that," the vice president says, grabbing my attention.

Before I can turn around to see what's going on, someone else begins to speak. A voice I haven't heard in eleven years. The voice I hoped I wouldn't hear today. *It's him.*

It's Thad.

Where'd he come from? I gulp, stomach churning. I haven't seen him yet tonight. Trust me, my eyes ran a marathon examining this entire place before I even sat down. I'm always on the lookout for someone who might know me. If I ever tell you that I didn't see you, but you saw me, I'm lying. I see everything.

"I wanted to say something," he states as the vice president attempts to reclaim the mic from his grip, but Thad manages to yank the mic back. "Please, just give me a couple minutes."

He has the attention of the entire room. And while everyone looks back and forth in confusion between Thad and the vice president, he starts speaking. *Where is this going?* I look around the room again. He had his own group of friends in high school, so why does he need everyone's attention when he can just talk to them?

I decide not to return to my seat yet. I don't want to catch his attention. Or anyone else's. Being invisible at the bar is safer.

"There's something I need to say." He looks around, face turning red. "There's something I didn't do a long time ago. And someone I need to say a few things to."

The cramping in the pit of my stomach becomes worse, and for a terrifying moment I think I'm going to have a *severe ass explosion*: a term only my mom and her best friends use. You know the feeling when your stomach is about to flush through you? Yeah, *that* feeling.

"Junior year, on the last day of school, I approached one of our classmates in the parking lot. And I tried to become friends with..."

As he speaks, I am immediately taken back to eleven years ago. It feels like I'm actually there. A place and time I never want to see again, yet a memory that has chosen to appear in my dreams throughout the years.

WEDNESDAY 04 JUNE 2008

2

LAST DAY OF JUNIOR YEAR

"Hey. Étienne," he said from the top of the school parking lot, behind me.

Guess I did hear steps.

I turned and looked up to see who it was. Well, I knew who it was. I'd known that voice for years. A masculine yet soft voice. I'd never heard it directed toward me, though. Well, at least not in that tone.

"Yeah?" I replied then looked around, thinking there had to be another Étienne standing not far from me. I did—and still do —that sometimes when people call my name and I'm not sure if it's me they're actually addressing. Like when someone waves in your direction, and the pitiful person inside you waves back without verifying who it is first. Then you're the idiot waving at no one. Yeah, I'm the awkward clown you get secondhand embarrassment for when you see this happen.

"Hey. I'm Thad." He smiled. He'd gotten his braces off the previous year, making his smile look like something you'd see on an Abercrombie & Fitch shopping bag.

"As if I didn't already know your name," I whispered to myself as he approached. We'd gone to the same schools and had been in the same classes since the fourth grade. *I know who you are. But I have to say, I'm surprised you know my name.*

"Yeah. Hey," I replied, scratching my left ear.

"You're here late." He looked around the nearly empty school parking lot, biting his lip as the light breeze lifted his ultra-blond hair.

"Oh. I had a cross country meeting," I replied. "We were going over our training schedule for mid-summer before classes start again in the fall."

Like I would have time to train over the summer, though. Some of us had to work. Luckily, summer conditioning wasn't actually mandatory, although it did help with my early season meets the last year. I wanted to train. Spending four days a week running up and down the lakeside, getting lost to the music on my iPod, would have been a better distraction than having to work.

"Need a ride home?" he asked, both hands now in his front pockets.

I looked frantically to see if anyone was around to observe this interaction. Was this a joke? Or a prank? Had he followed me? Was he waiting for me? I hesitated to reply. I needed time to think. Was this guy really trying to be nice or was this a setup by him and his group of friends?

"Umm sure," I stuttered. I only lived a block away, after all. What harm could it do?

"Cool! I'm parked right there," he replied, his voice strangely enthusiastic.

I looked toward his car, side-eyeing him in confusion as my heart fluttered. *Hold on. What was that?*

His car was in the last row of the parking lot, facing the tall fencing separating the school grounds and the back yards of the people living on the next street over. My street. When no one was around I would usually climb the fence to my backyard. That day, like so many others, I'd decided to exit through the parking lot to take the long way home to get lost in my music, and to avoid the chaos at my house.

"Long Way Home" by ATB was one of my favorite songs, so I decided I would listen to that album on my walk. I liked taking the long way, anyway. I felt alone, and this song made me feel good, like being alone wasn't such a bad thing.

After a moment of me twiddling my thumbs in his parked Focus, an electric feeling overcame me. Like butterflies in my stomach, but not in that way. I thought. More like nervousness had enveloped my being. I had ventured into the unknown and now had to see what would come next.

"How was the last day of school for you?" he asked before adding, "Funny how our last day is always on a Wednesday."

I sat there concentrating on my peripheral to catch any movement. *People need to see this. Where are they? Why is this guy, of all people, talking to me?*

"Fine. Yours?" I replied, trying to give away as little as I could. *I mean, I've wanted to know you for years and here we are. In your car. On this hot day.*

Speaking of hot, I wanted to open the window, but he still hadn't started the car. What was I supposed to do? Open the door for some air and feel more ridiculously awkward?

"It was." His voice cracked. "Fine. You know?"

I nodded, looking at his fidgeting hands in his lap.

"I made some plans for next week and hung out with my friends during the fifth period assembly," he continued, talking to me as if we were friends.

He'd never seemed like the friendly type before. Was this nervousness pushing him to talk? Or was he genuinely a kind person? All these years of receiving the silent treatment from him had me confused.

Like the last time I made eye contact with him in the hallway at my locker, only the week before. At my locker, I turned my head and immediately noticed him from my peripheral, turning the corner and heading my way. I looked up too quickly, flinging my contact lenses out of focus, which forced an awkward scowl on my face as I blinked to refocus. I usually tried to grin after making eye contact with someone. But my contact lenses had other plans. My vision cleared, and our eyes met for a moment as he bit both of his lips. He quickly redirected his gaze past me to the end of the hall and kept on his merry way.

I assumed he was one of those *popular* types who spoke only to those who *mattered*, like once in American Government when we were assigned to the same group, discussing the pros and cons of Don't Ask, Don't Tell. He sat there tapping his pencil, staring at the blackboard. Had I been wrong all this time?

"Hey," I blurted into the weird silence after he finished telling me about his last period. I felt dizzy from the heat building up in the car. We were shaded by a tree branch peeking out over the fence, but June heat in Michigan could be a killer even in the shade. Well, at least in those years before the climate was drastically changing. "Could you maybe start the car or open a window?"

I was still wondering what the hell I was doing in Thad's car. Thad, of all people.

"Ooh." He twitched, hands reaching for the keys that fell from his lap onto the floor. "They're right, you're easy to talk to."

Who's they? A cloud of anxiety fell over me. *People talk about me? Why?* I had tried so hard in life to blend in, why were people talking about me?

He grinned after finally turning on his car and blasting the air conditioning. "So. What are you up to today?"

I grabbed my chest, looking around even though I was obviously the only one in the car. "Uh. Me?"

His eyes met mine as he clenched his jaw. "Yeah. I was thinking..."

"Hold on." I raised my hands. Thad straightened himself as

if trying to take a step backward, but obviously we were both confined in the car. "What's going on here?" What I really wanted to say was, *Why are you talking to me? You've barely spoken to me before.*

"What do you mean? Nothing's going on." He looked down. "Look, I don't know why I asked to drive you home. I just..." He didn't continue.

"I have a hard time believing that," I said. *Shit!* I said that. It forced itself out of me like word vomit. I mean, I *did* have a hard time believing that someone like him, someone who had never really spoken to me, would pick up a conversation and offer me a ride home. But I was usually better at controlling my urges and keeping thoughts to myself. "Sorry. What I meant to say—"

"I know what you meant."

"I'm sorry. We've been in the same classes together for the last seven years and have never exchanged more than a few words. I'm not trying to be rude. Some people aren't who they say they are."

He turned his head slightly, revealing a half grin.

I thought I had a point, though. I decided a long time ago to become a wallflower and keep myself away from the shitty drama of high school. People were your friends one minute, then the next you weren't cool enough for them anymore. I only had one real friend. Yeah, a few girls sat with me during lunch every day, but my only true friend was Dana.

"I know," he said, resting his right arm on the center console. He then stretched out his arm. "Let's start over then. Hey, I'm Thad."

I reached my hand out to shake his and felt more confused than ever. My uneasiness faded, though, as he grasped my hand firmly with his. But then fear decided to emerge as I realized how cold my hands were. How cold they must feel to another person. To him.

That's a physical trait I've never understood. No matter how warm the weather is, or how heated I feel after a run, my hands are always cold. Dana would tell me it was because I was dead inside, which always made me laugh. But my mom, being a mom, would tell me it was because the warmth was concentrated in my heart. Her response forced my eyes to roll far back into my head every time she said it.

"I'm Étienne," I stated as a matter of fact. I was probably the only person in our school with that name.

"What do you like to do for fun, Étienne? Actually, let's get out of here." He switched gears to back out of the spot.

"Well, I um. I can only go home. Like you offered," I said, my voice louder than I intended, as the fear of being seen with him crept over me.

The car suddenly stopped. "Huh?"

"I have to get home. I have to go to work for a few hours," I said, but it was a lie. I was too scared to see where this was going. He was acting too friendly to say *Let's get out of here*, like he wasn't actually planning on taking me home.

"Oh. Where do you work?"

I shrugged. "Just at this jewelry store down Harper."

"Want me to drive you there?"

"No. Thank you. I need to get home and change. Then I'll take my mom's car," I replied. I had my license, but not enough money to get my own car. My mom would have found a way to pitch in and get me a cheap car, but I didn't want to add the extra stress.

"Okay. Here. Give me your phone." He reached out.

I pulled my phone out of my back-right pocket and handed it over. It's funny how different the phones used to be compared to the massive-screened smart phones of today. Mine at the time was the Sidekick in midnight blue. It was kind of useless since my mom wouldn't pay for the internet service, but I really wanted it for the cool sliding screen and full keyboard. It made texting so much easier than using T9 on flip phones. I'd never

forgotten that phone. It was a gift from my dad before he—
Well, I'm not getting into that with you just yet.

He slid the screen open and added his number into the contacts, then handed it back to me as my thoughts ran a thousand miles an hour.

There was a problem with that. He didn't call or text himself. Which meant he didn't have mine, leaving me with the arduous and terrifying task of having to contact him first. *Why?* I asked myself after putting the phone back in my pocket. Why was I the one who had to contact him? Was this a test? I could have him take me home and I would forget the number was ever there. That's what I would do. I would forget about this and hopefully he would too by the time senior year started in the fall.

But then I'd be the ass who ditched him. I'd be the person he and his friends, and eventually everyone else, thought was the inconsiderate jerk. Not that I really cared what people said about me.

As he made a right turn out of the parking lot and onto the main road, he asked if I wanted to hang out after my shift.

"Um. I can't," I replied.

"K. I get it." There was that dreaded *K*.

"No. You don't. I have plans with my friend Dana after I get off work." I was still apprehensive about this whole encounter, and he knew—I could see in his eyes.

"Oh," he said, the pitch of his voice ascending. "Well, then, tomorrow?" His eyes widened.

I looked at his face as he gazed toward the stoplight before making a turn onto my street. He didn't look as intimidating as I thought he'd be. There was something in there. Something in those eyes soothed my continuous doubt. Did I like this guy? Was it safe for me to let him in?

"Woah!" He threw his arm toward my chest, stopping me from suddenly jolting forward as he pressed on the brakes.

My eyes widened as I exhaled from the light pressure of his

arm, adrenaline beating through my chest. The silver Grand Caravan in front of us had stopped too quickly just before my street. *How did he not see that car? Was he not paying attention?* Our eyes met, and the adrenaline turned into butterflies.

"Shit. Sorry." He put his right hand back on the wheel, cheeks red.

I nodded, then looked forward to calm my body as he turned onto my street. My house was halfway to the next main road so I had time to catch my breath before getting inside and being questioned.

He slowed down a few houses before mine. "So, tomorrow?" he hesitantly asked again.

I looked at my house slowly approaching to the right, the bleachers of the football field towering behind the three houses before mine. "Alrighty. Yeah, we can do that."

He looked forward and smiled with an air of accomplishment, his red cheeks returning to their pinkish color.

Does he like me? He can't like me. People at this school don't like me like that. I side-eyed him, reaching down for my backpack.

"See ya later, Étienne," I heard faintly before closing the door.

I pretended I didn't hear it and waved as I walked up the driveway, but I definitely heard it. I also heard the tone of his voice. Like he was looking forward to it. *What's going on?* I thought. I really didn't understand what had happened. Were we friends? Did he like me? Was this a trick?

I turned and looked up the driveway to the green metal gate, wishing I understood what just happened. And wishing I had taken the long way home as I intended.

A few moments later I found myself sitting on my bed with my headphones in, listening to OceanLab's new single "Sirens of the Sea" to try to mute the thoughts going through my head. I couldn't stop replaying the conversation with Thad. I didn't understand what encouraged him to approach me. *Am I an interesting person? Yeah, that's a no.* Did he need something from me but didn't want to be too forward and ask? *That's what it is. He needed something from me.*

But what could it be? I asked myself before the door flew open.

"Really, Callum?" I threw my hands up as my kid brother entered, his twin Niall trailing behind him.

"Where's my walkie talkie?" he demanded, turning over my hamper while Niall started pulling stuff out from under my bed.

"What are you—*get out* from under there." I pulled on Niall's stubby leg after he shoved out my swim bag. "Don't you have another one?" I shook my head, still firmly holding on to Niall's ankle.

"Étienne. Let go! We both have one," replied Niall.

"I can't find mine. It's gotta be in here," Callum said, opening my closet door.

"Out! Get out. You shouldn't have been in my room in the first place. Go bother Riley. I'm not in the mood." I pointed to the door.

"Whatever, butthead." Callum let go of the closet door handle and followed his twin out of my room.

Butthead? What is he, seven? I grabbed my iPod and head-phones that had fallen on the floor when I jumped up and grabbed Niall's leg.

And yes, those were my siblings' names. My mother decided to give them all Irish names. Creative, right? My mom named my sister Riley, then my brothers Callum and Niall since my dad wouldn't let her name me—his first child was a son, and he wanted to name his firstborn son. My mom relied on her Irish ancestry to name them, though she wasn't connected to her heritage. I didn't mind my sister, though. The twins were the youngest so she and I always got along pretty well, being the older siblings. As for my name, what's funny is that my dad decided to give me a French name—something completely removed from his Middle Eastern heritage. I mean, how did a proud Lebanese, chain-smoking immigrant named Yousef not give any of his children Arabic names?

Later, I decided to take my dog Frankie out for a walk to blow off some steam before hanging out with Dana.

I couldn't get Thad out of my mind. This had never happened to me. People didn't come up out of nowhere trying to be my friend. Especially a guy. I didn't have guy friends. Guys weren't interested in being familiar with me. I only ever appealed to girls, but not in that way. Girls liked to talk to me. They would tell me all about their boyfriends and their secrets, which I think is why most guys left me alone. I guess I was lucky. Maybe they were afraid I knew too much about them.

Wait. I stopped at the end of my block, looking at the tall, bricked post that marked the crosswalk. Frankie's long sausage body stretched out on the patch of grass at the corner of the sidewalk. He needed to sit for a second to rest while we waited for traffic to clear. "Is this just an advance for Thad? Is he trying to get close to me, to get closer to a girl I know?" I asked myself, out loud this time.

Yes. If you want to know, I talk to myself quite often. Not just thinking, I actually talk to myself when I'm not around people who can hear. It helps me concentrate on what I'm thinking so everything isn't jumbled in my head. You're starting to get a glimpse inside of it. You understand, right?

"Am I overthinking this? Maybe he's a nice person who wants to be friends with me. Yeah, probably not." I sighed, looking to the main road as the traffic cleared. I nudged my long-bodied dog, and we crossed the main road to walk down another block.

Oh god. What will Dana think of this?

3

———

DANA

I returned from my walk with Frankie before nine o'clock. My family had already eaten dinner. My twin brothers were thankfully in bed since the elementary schools didn't go on summer break for another week. Riley was probably in her room texting her boyfriend. And my mom was watching TV with her mom in the rear living room.

"Hey Tony. Where were you? You missed dinner," my mom yelled as she heard me searching the fridge for some leftovers.

"Ma! My name is Étienne."

"Brenda. His name is not Tony," my grandma added, sticking up for me as she usually does.

I closed the fridge door for a second to look down at the ugly brown, orange, and tan linoleum floor. Memories of my mom calling me anything other than Étienne floating around like video snippets.

Tony—the name my mother wanted to give me, and my father forbade. She picked out the names before she even met my dad. She always tried to use Tony as my nickname throughout the years, but he usually stopped her. After he was gone, she tried to use it less, but it slipped out here and there.

"Ugh. Okay, Étienne. Where were you? You missed dinner," she shouted again. I heard the jingling of Frankie's tags as he ran toward her. "Oh, and I made extra salad," she added.

"Thanks, Ma. I went for a walk with Frankie. Needed to clear my head," I yelled, carefully pulling the Pyrex salad bowl out of the fridge as I lifted the container of baked Kibbeh on top of it, almost wishing I hadn't recently become vegetarian.

The salad was delicious, though. My mom made this Mediterranean salad made up of cucumbers, tomatoes, kalamata olives, and a simple lemon and garlic vinaigrette. The garlicy and lemony smell of the dressing usually made me salivate when she put everything together. I know how to make it as well, but nothing is ever as good as your mom's food. No matter who you are.

My phone dinged as I inhaled the salad. *Hey. On my way.* It was Dana, my best friend.

Shit, I thought, trying to satisfy my hunger fast enough to give me enough time to change my clothes.

Alrighty, I replied, bolting to the bathroom to brush my teeth. And before I had the chance to check my hair in the mirror, there was a thump at the back door. I threw on some jeans and glanced in the mirror one more time to make sure I looked somewhat presentable.

"Dana's here," Niall yelled as I heard both of the twins' footsteps approaching.

Ugh. I thought they were in bed.

"Ooh, trying to look fancy huh? You like Dana, don't you?" Callum winked, tilting his head to the side.

"Get out of here. Aren't you both supposed to be in bed?" I shoved them out of the doorway.

"Étienne's got a girlfriend. Étienne's got a girlfriend," they said in unison, running to their shared bedroom.

If only they knew.

"Hey," Dana said as she approached the bathroom where I

was still staring in the mirror. "Your hair looks fine, Étienne. Stop obsessing." She leaned up against the doorframe.

"I'm not obsessing. It doesn't do what I want it to do like yours does." I pointed to her newly dyed orange hair.

Dana's hair was nothing like mine. It was straight, never frizzy, and naturally blonde. Though her parents let her do whatever she wanted with her hair, which she took advantage of very frequently.

"Whatever. Let's go for a drive." She turned toward the blue couch in our front sitting room.

I fiddled with my hair for another minute before grabbing a cardigan. Then I grabbed my house keys and tapped her on the shoulder, meaning I was heading toward the back door. Thankfully Dana had her own car.

"Be home before midnight, Étienne," my mom yelled from the rear living room. It was probably going to be longer than that, though.

When I was in high school, she usually trusted me to do the right thing. I could go anywhere and stay out as late as I wanted, as long as my chores were done, and I answered her prying questions upon returning home. She gave me rules when I wanted to go out, but it was usually a formality so my siblings wouldn't get jealous thinking she had a favorite.

"Bye, Ma," I said as Dana and I hurried out the back door to her car parked in the driveway.

"Ahh." Dana sighed after she started the car. "I love your mom," she said, looking behind her as she backed out of the driveway.

"Take her," I joked before adding, "So. Where to?"

Dana decided we would drive down Jefferson Avenue to catch the freshwater breeze before figuring out where we were going to end up. I opened my passenger side window.

"Hey, can you roll down the other windows?" I asked.

She opened all of the windows, including the moonroof.

And I could finally let go of all my anxieties and breathe. We sat there in silence, cruising down the avenue hugging the coastline of Lake St. Clair. The horizon was a dark blue to the east of us, and I could see a few stars above the water in the distance to the left. The moon and all its wisdom hung above us through the opened roof of Dana's gray Escape; I laid my head back to admire it. I've always loved staring at our moon. I wondered what it would be like to stare back at us, Earth, from the lunar surface. Would it be as pretty as observing the rocky imprints of ancient, violent collisions? Would we be able to see the detailed green coastlines crashing with the deep blue oceans?

With Dana, we could sit there for eternity in silence. We didn't have to talk while hanging out. She knew what I needed, and I the same for her. We didn't hang out every day like most best friends did. But we also didn't need to. Do you have a best friend like that?

"You seem really anxious today. What's going on?" She broke the silence, glancing over to me, her orange hair flying above the head rest. I wished the car swerved over the median and into the lake.

"What do you mean?" I replied casually. I didn't want her to know she caught me off guard. The reality was, I was clenching my jaw and squeezing my right thigh.

She did this on purpose. She knows something's up and waited for the perfect moment.

"Come on, Étienne. I know you." She lifted her hand for a second.

"Honestly, I'm fine. Just tired from the day." I kept my gaze forward, knowing she would see through my eyes if I looked at her directly.

"Yeah? What was tiring about the day? We literally had nothing to do at school except dodgeball with the lowerclassmen for personal fitness," she pushed. She could see I wasn't telling her something.

"This is really ruining the moment, you know," I spat out, crossing my arms as my voice cracked. My emotions began to seep through, like a leak at the end of a hose that hasn't been properly fastened to the faucet.

I tried hard to hide my emotions from others. People say that showing emotions is a sign of strength, but for me it felt like a sign of weakness. Especially when I was that age. Your words shouldn't have impacted me. If they did, I was weak enough to let you get the better of me.

I directed my eyes up at the sky through Dana's moonroof. She decided to turn around and head back toward town. And by the time I realized we were no longer by the water, we were in the parking lot of our old elementary school, the side bordering the playground past the back entrance.

"Let's go on the swing sets," Dana mumbled before exiting the car.

She slammed the driver door much harder than normal, her way of telling me that she was pissed and needed to blow off some steam. Maybe I needed it too. The adrenaline of the swings would put us both in a better mood.

It was strange being there. We hadn't frequented this specific playground in a long time, though we liked going to random playgrounds in the city to swing. It felt so much smaller than I remembered our old school being. Even the baseball diamond in the corner of the field looked awkwardly small. *How did we ever play kickball there?*

Dana and I met in the fourth grade here. I'd never forgotten how nervous I was to be starting at a new school. We hadn't met until after lunch during recess, as we weren't in the same class until fifth grade. When I got to the playground and saw everyone already huddled in their groups, I went to the swings, my favorite thing to do.

"Remember this?" she asked, pointing to the last two swings at the far end of the wood chipped area, before the grass went on for what felt like a mile when I was a kid, and ended at the fence.

"I do." I smiled, meeting her deep brown eyes.

The last two swings at the end of the row is exactly where we met. As I sat in the last one, she sat next to me after she and Samantha got into a fight. And we swung together, as high as we could, until recess was over. I don't think we said much, but we both loved it, and agreed we had to become friends. She was wild, fun and didn't take shit from anyone.

"My mom got us the tickets for Saturday," she said as we both spun in circles.

"Awesome. Thanks. I can't wait to go." I threw my legs up, spinning rapidly after twisting the chain as far as I could. "How much do I owe her again?"

"I don't remember. But she won't care if you forget to pay her back."

"Ask her, though."

"I won't forget. Won't it be fun next year to go on Senior Skip Day and not have to wait in the lines since everyone will still be in school?"

"I hope so. But do other schools do Senior Skip Day at Cedar Point too?"

"Does it really matter?"

"I guess not." I shrugged.

"Where did you go after personal fitness today? I waited to walk back to our lockers."

"Oh. I felt sick and ran to the bathroom," I said. But that was a lie.

"Everything all right?"

I wanted to say no. But I nodded instead.

It was a good last day of school, until personal fitness ended and one of the lowerclassmen whispered, "I didn't know Arab fags existed," under his breath as he passed me. And there was no reason to talk about it with Dana. She would have flipped like when in sixth grade someone told me to go bomb myself. Wouldn't you have flipped if you were my friend in those moments?

Those comments happened here and there, especially in fifth grade and when we entered middle school, not long after 9/11. But I usually ignored them. My mom would tell me those kids didn't know what they were talking about and were repeating the words of their bigoted, uneducated parents. My mom isn't Arab, but since her kids are, she found herself having to defend us.

"You sure something's not up?" she whispered.

I nodded and shrugged in response. She could read me better than anyone else could, and I was hiding something—from her, my best friend. Why? I couldn't put the words together to tell you. Her reaction to what happened with Thad and me might not be what I hoped, so I was scared to tell her. She didn't officially know I was gay. I think *I* even had problems admitting it to myself. What if she didn't accept me? What would I do if my own best friend rejected me? But for the first time in my life, a guy wanted to be my friend. So it seemed. And I wanted that.

"Fine. I'll tell you something, then. But you have to at least give me something in return when I'm done."

"Fine." I shook my head, frantically trying to think of something, flipping through responses like a rolodex.

Dana explained that she started seeing someone two weeks earlier, after our weekend at Movement, a music festival we both attended.

"Wait, hold on. The night you told me to go ahead and leave, and that you got a ride home?" I had driven us in my mom's car.

"Yeah. I went home with him. Well, he had a hotel room a few blocks away," she replied with an air of, *Yeah, so. Who cares?*

"Dana! You went home with and hooked up with someone you met at a festival?"

She winked, a sly grin appearing on her mouth.

"Are you kidding me? You could've been killed. Or worse," I tried to continue, but she tilted her head and gave me the *Stop now* look.

My secret seems way less important now, I thought.

"How old is he? Dana. We literally just turned seventeen. What if he's a gross twenty-five-year-old looking to prey on you?"

"My god Étienne, chill out. He's the same age as us and lives like ten miles away," she replied, trying to ease my bewilderment.

"But how'd he get a hotel room if he's the same age as us?" I sighed heavily.

"Étienne. Like any of us would. Just ask someone you know older than eighteen. Plus, it's Detroit. No one cares."

"Why are you telling me about this now, then?" I demanded. As if I had the right to ask her when I wasn't telling her what was going on with me.

"Uh, well I think I really like him, I guess. We hung out a few times this last week."

"What's his name?"

"James. We were dancing together when you went to grab food and I gave him my number when you texted me to come eat."

She went on to talk more about him—where he went to school, and what they had been doing together. As she went further into detail, it made me realize I was being a coward. She was brave enough to tell me her secret. What was I waiting for? She was my best friend, after all.

What are you so afraid of, Étienne? Just tell her. It's not a big deal.

I took in a breath, about to tell Dana what was going on inside my head. My meeting with Thad earlier that day. How he asked to hang out. How I was feeling about it. I opened my mouth, trying to keep my end of her deal, but instead something else came out.

"Let's see who can jump the farthest." I started pumping back and forth to gain speed on the swing. She immediately jumped up and threw her legs toward the sky.

Yes. I was a coward, but I guess self-defense and self-preservation proved more important than being honest with my best friend.

"Hey! Hold on," she bellowed.

I continued pumping my legs, getting higher and higher as Dana caught up to me. My head turned toward the dark sky, the chain starting to buckle and tighten as I ascended, then descended. I searched for the moon as I reached higher and higher, while a sinking feeling in my stomach appeared as if I were on a roller coaster.

"Hey," said Dana, cutting off my search.

"What?"

"Ready? Three, two..."

I turned my head forward and readied my arms as we prepared to jump. I let go of the chains as my legs straightened, preparing for the impact. But my left foot found an unwanted depression in the wood chips, and I stumbled in my landing.

"Ha! You suck." Dana clearly won the contest with her superior athletic abilities, and thankfully dropped the fact that I was supposed to say something.

After nearly spraining my left ankle trying to land on the rough mulch, I headed back with Dana to her house where we could relax in her family's back porch jacuzzi.

"Hey T." I wasn't sure why Dana's mom called me T, but I was okay with it. She was one of those cool moms.

"I feel like I haven't seen you in ages. Where've you been? How'd the end of the semester treat ya?" she asked while opening the fridge to grab a beer.

"It was ehh. You know." I shrugged then threw myself onto the floor to give the family's chocolate Lab some kisses.

I didn't much enjoy classes at my school. Well, I don't think many people do. The required subjects weren't too exciting. I only enjoyed after the day ended and I had practice for an hour and a half. At least then I knew what was expected of me.

I ran and grabbed my bathing suit from Dana's room—yes, I kept a bathing suit there—then ran into her older brother's room to change. Normally I would have gone into the bathroom to change but her brother's room sat right across from hers and he wasn't home.

Dana and I met in the hallway. She wore a neon purple two-piece, her orange hair piled on the top of her head in a messy bun. Me in my sapphire swim trunks, holding my back straight as a board and sucking my stomach in as my dad taught me.

Dana's mom lifted up her beer as we passed through the kitchen on our way to the back door. "Want one?"

"Sure. Ope. Étienne, let me scooch past ya," Dana said as she wiggled between me and the kitchen island.

"How about you?" Dana's mom pointed to me.

"Yeah, I guess." I clenched my jaw, unsure if I should.

"Only one though!" She pointed at the two of us before adding, "You can enjoy yourselves under my roof, but only so much. You're still teenagers."

Understandable, I thought to myself.

"Oh. And close the gate so she doesn't get out. I'm going to leave 'er in the yard with you guys for a while," her mom said, pointing to their family dog.

I wonder what I'll be like then. I closed the backyard gate as I looked past the kitchen window into the living room. Would I be a cool, laid-back parent like Dana's or a strict one? Would I even be able to have kids? If so, I hoped to be better than some of the examples I had seen. My mom was pretty cool, though sometimes a little gossipy. Most of the people I knew in school either had terribly strict parents, or parents who didn't give a shit about them. What were yours like?

Dana and I climbed into the jacuzzi, and as the bubbles

began to form a cloud of warm air around us, I felt my anxieties start to drift away along with the pain in my left ankle. It was nice to sit there and not think of anything while we sipped on the cold beer.

"Hey there," I said once Dana's mom let the dog out.

"Hey girly." Dana reached her arm out. Her dog stood on the deck, body and neck stretched down toward the water as Dana shifted in her direction.

"So," Dana began, then she sipped her beer and stopped for a second, leaving room for my dreaded thoughts to tiptoe back into sight. My memories of that afternoon with Thad bashed against the sides of my head.

"Tell me something," she said, then paused before adding, "since you're obviously not going to tell me what the hell is wrong with you today, answer this question."

I closed my eyes for a second and gulped as if I were looking at a long needle coming toward me, sitting in the health clinic with my mom and siblings awaiting our yearly vaccinations. Then I nodded.

"Are *you* seeing anyone?"

My stomach ascended as if I were dropping from the tallest peak of the Millennium Force roller coaster. I don't know why I was so nervous. I wasn't seeing anyone. Thad wasn't even my friend yet.

"No." My eyes looked to the side quickly.

"Oh come on! You never tell me anything. You've never once told me about anyone you like. You've got to like someone," she insisted.

"It's nothing. I promise there's nothing wrong today. I'm tired."

"Mhmm yeah okay, bullshit. Like I believe that."

"Dana. I'm not interested in anyone. Really. And even if I were, I'm not really the type of person people are interested in," I stuttered, realizing it probably was true.

I genuinely didn't think people liked me like that. I had never once been asked out. I don't even think anyone had ever actually flirted with me, other than play flirting with Dana and a few other girls at our lunch table.

"Bullshit. Why would you say that, Étienne? Of course people like you. You're like the only guy in school who actually puts himself together every day."

"Then why does no one ever show interest in me?" I blurted out unintentionally.

"Argh. Étienne." She threw her hands up. "People *are* interested in you. You're too self-conscious to see it. You're literally in your own world most of the time. Sometimes I even hear you whispering to yourself."

That was true. I did talk to myself a lot. And I did daydream a lot. But I mean seriously, were people really interested in me?

Dana continued, "You need to open yourself more and stop hiding in the shadow of me and our friends. Just talk to people. Reach out. Loosen up."

I glanced over at her, then inhaled.

"The only reason we're friends is because I forced you to talk to me that day on the swings," she added.

There is truth to that.

"Okay. Fine," I said before adding, "maybe there is someone I like. But I don't know if they like me. And I'm not telling you who it might be yet." That was terrifying to say. And I made sure to not specify the gender. I didn't think Dana would care, but I wasn't ready to share yet. The fact is, I didn't actually like anyone, but it was the only way of getting her off my back.

"Finally," she groaned, taking a gulp of her beer before adding, "you finally fucking said something."

Maybe I should stop being such a brooder and talk to people. I took a sip of the beer.

Dana and I ended up having two beers each after her mom

went to bed, so I decided to walk home and not take a chance in having her drive me.

As I walked home, a calming feeling flowed through my body, probably due to the alcohol in my system. I usually only took sips from my mom's vodka and sprite after dinner while she watched reruns of *ER*. It was really late by the time I got home —or really early, since it was the next day. Instead of going into the house and risking the loud creak from the side door, I decided to lie in my sister's hammock hanging between the only tree in our backyard and a hook she installed on the side of the garage.

Hopefully that hook will hold, I thought, looking up as I climbed in and flung my left leg out of the side. I lay there for a moment, then heard a faint raspy bark from inside the house. *Dammit, Frankie. You're going to wake everyone.*

I jumped out of the hammock and opened the door as slowly as possible to avoid the creaking. "Come on, Frankie. Go potty," I whispered as he sniffed the grass. He didn't want to go, though. He wanted to be outside with me, his usual nighttime partner. I grabbed him and placed him on my chest once I re-entered the hammock.

Lying there and looking up at the dark sky made me think of all the possibilities that came to be our existence. There could be another being out there staring back and thinking the same thing. Interesting, right? I often thought about how another world could be out there. One better than ours. How could there not be other inhabited planets out there looking up at the sky? There's so much out there.

The moon was still visible through the tree branches to my right. "I wonder what it'd be like to go there," I said to myself, caressing Frankie's long back.

A thought popped into my mind. Not so much a thought, but a name. His name.

I pulled my phone from the back-right pocket of my jeans

and flipped it open. Looked through my contacts and there it was. His name. Exactly where he put it the day before. And as I sat there thinking about him and everything he said to me, Dana's voice popped into my mind. *"Just talk to people. Reach out."* What harm could it do? I only wanted to make a friend.

Hey. It's Étienne, I texted.

And after almost an hour of staring at my phone, there was no response.

It's the middle of the night, Étienne. Go to bed, you idiot. "Come on Frankie. Let's go to bed."

THURSDAY 05 JUNE 2008

4

REALLY, RILEY?

B*oom!*
Niall kicked open the door and Callum ran in and jumped on top of me.

"What the—"

My twin brothers pulled the blanket off me and shouted in unison, "Where were you last night, Étienne?"

"Argh, what time is it?" I shrieked as Niall joined Callum in squishing me on my bed. "Watch out, you goons. Frankie's under the covers with me." I frantically felt for the long sausage body, but he wasn't there. *Whew.* I reached out and grabbed my phone from the nightstand. *7:45* it read.

"Ugh, aren't you idiots supposed to be on the way to school?"

"Callum. Niall. Go get changed now! We're leaving in ten minutes whether you're dressed or not," my mom yelled from the kitchen.

Thankfully that was their cue to leave the room, but not before yelling out in unison, "Étienne's got a girlfriend. Étienne's got a girlfriend."

They really have no idea, do they?

I slammed the door shut after they ran out. Then I lay back in bed with a pillow over my face to try to get some more sleep.

Wait. Did he text me back?

I tore the pillow off my face and leaned over to check my phone again. *Hmm.* No response. Was it too early in the morning? Or was he avoiding me after our strange encounter the day before? Maybe he was thinking the same thing I was: *Why am I so eager to talk to this guy?* Or worse. He could be asking himself why I texted him so late at night.

My hand involuntarily reached for the pillow and threw it back on my face as the thoughts began to deepen and my anxiety from the previous day spiked. Again.

"Hey," Riley yelled from the bathroom across the hall. "Étienne."

"Ergh, do you not see what time it is, Riley? Why are you up so early?"

"Good morning to you too. Sheesh," she replied. "Do you work tonight? I might need you to drive me to Nate's when Mom gets off work. She told me to walk. What kind of mom tells her daughter to walk?"

"No. I requested the day off weeks ago so I could sleep. You know it's summer break now? We can sleep in!" I shook my head before adding, "Just walk. He lives like less than a half mile from here."

"Come on. Please. Just drop me off when Mom gets home from work."

"Riley! You know Mom literally uses her car for work. She can't just waste her gas money on you needing a ride to Nate's."

My mom was a visiting nurse. It was a hard job, but she liked that she could set her own hours and take days off when she needed to. She had suggested I look into it since I did so well taking care of my dad. And I didn't know what I wanted to do with my life. I gave it a shot, shadowing one of my mom's nurse friends during spring break. But it wasn't for me.

"You've been such a downer lately, Étienne. Please?"

"When have I been a downer?" I cocked my head up.

"Uh, look at you."

"Whatever. I can't. I don't know if I'll be home later," I replied, still thinking about the text message. I was telling the truth. What if he did respond and wanted to hang out? I wouldn't be able to drive her. Then again, what if he didn't?

"Fine," I told her. "But you have to be ready as soon as she gets home. And feed Frankie right now, please."

"All right. What's got you all wound up?" she whispered loud enough for me to hear.

I got up and closed the door again, this time throwing a bunch of books in front of it to keep it closed. The bedroom doors had been painted so many times over the years that they didn't shut properly and cracked open without you knowing.

I lay on the bed for another hour without being able to fall back to sleep, then decided to get up. I needed to do my laundry anyway.

Seriously? She can walk, I said to myself as I passed my sister with the laundry basket in my hands. She was on her way out the door to walk to her girlfriend's house a block away. *If you can walk a block, you can walk a few more blocks to get to Nate's.*

I spent some time in the basement sorting through my hamper to see what needed to go in the delicate cycle, and what could wait for the permanent press afterward.

Yes. As a teenager I did my own laundry and sorted my clothes according to what the tag said. I've always been particular about how my clothes fit—slim but not tight. Especially after my mom ruined one of my favorite polos in the dryer. From then on, no one was ever allowed to touch my clothes.

My phone dinged as I walked up the steps to the kitchen. *Heyy.* I nearly dropped the laundry basket.

It's him!

My stomach fell upward into my throat as if I had woken up

from a falling dream. There the message was, just below mine from much earlier. *Ugh, how am I going to respond to "Heyy"?* I stood still, looking around to make sure no one was around me. Yes, I was alone in the house, but when you have three younger siblings, there are always prying eyes. And as I began to think of how to respond, the side door opened, bringing in the sound of multiple teenage voices giggling and whispering.

Shit. I was supposed to be alone for a couple hours.

"Étienne, you still home?" my sister asked. She turned the corner and saw me standing at the top of the steps in the kitchen. "Ugh. You know you look like a creep standing there all quiet and waiting."

"Really, Riley?"

"Nate's dad picked us all up. We're going to hang out here for the day. Don't worry about later."

Don't worry about later? I'm worrying about right now. How can I think while you guys are here making a bunch of noise?

My sister, her boyfriend, and two of her friends invaded the rear living room, forcing me to hide out in my bedroom and try to think of how to respond to this message without sounding too eager. And to obviously examine why he would use the letter *y* twice in *Heyy*.

I wasn't sure of what to say. Did I want to be the one to initiate a meetup or did I want to tell him I texted to provide my number? I didn't want him to think I was too keen on seeing him. Wasn't I, though?

But then what if I came off as rude by not asking to hang out? What if he thought, *He's texting me to tell me I have his number now? Is this a joke? Forget it.*

It shouldn't have been this hard to reply to a text message. I just wanted a friend who wasn't a girl. I'd never had one before. Was that so much to ask for? I was awkward and quiet around my male peers. Too awkward. Too quiet.

After several minutes thinking about how to ask if he

wanted to hang out, I realized how early I had texted him. *I'm such a creep! Why did I text him so early? What is wrong with you, Étienne?*

So, instead of initiating a meetup, I decided to apologize. *Hey. Sorry for the early text. I was up really late and forgot what time it was.*

I sat, looking at the message for a few minutes with my thumb on send, then thought about erasing it to calm down and see if he would send me another message. I was about to close my phone and grab my iPod to lose myself in the trancey beats of Paul Van Dyk's album *Global* when my door flew open.

"What the— Come on, Riley. I could've been changing or something."

She rolled her eyes. "Seriously? It's not like I haven't seen you before, Étienne."

"No you haven't!" I said. She had when we were kids, like all siblings do when they're really young. But definitely not as teenagers. Even before that. I always made it a point that people not see me without clothes on. Well, unless I was wearing a bathing suit to swim. But that's different.

My siblings paid no attention to privacy. They didn't care who did or didn't see them unclothed in their own house. Even as Riley aged and started to become more self-aware, she'd slip here and there. Like when I was sitting in the rear living room with my mom and her friend Laura watching TV, probably *The Real Housewives* of something. Riley came to the room in a bathrobe with her hair wrapped in a towel. She didn't want to be left out of seeing the episode. So she grabbed her long mirror, which usually leaned against the wall in her room next to the closet, and sat on the couch next to me, holding the mirror upright with her left hand as she did her makeup with the right. She told us she needed to adjust her bathrobe and to look down so we wouldn't see anything, so my mom, Laura, and I looked down to give her some privacy. Finished, Riley placed the mirror on the floor, and before she said it was okay to look up, she decided to step over the mirror.

My crazy sister stepped over the damn mirror while we were looking down. Who does that?

"What do you want?" I looked at Riley in the doorway.

"Can we plug your iPod into the speakers?" she replied.

"Ugh, what for?"

"To watch TV." She slapped the door then added, "Come on. You've got good music on yours. Please Étienne, I never ask you for anything."

Never ask me for anything. That's a lie. "All right. But I'll be the one to plug it in and put something on. I don't want your friends' gross hands greasing up my stuff." I can't handle people who don't wash their hands regularly. Like, is it that hard to keep yourself clean?

"Okay. Whatever."

"I'll be out in a minute," I said as I waved at her to leave my room. I went to the bedside table to grab my iPod from the drawer and noticed my Sidekick screen was still flipped open. Riley had stopped me from erasing the message I was about to send.

"Shit." A blanket of fear fell over me. I accidentally hit send when Riley opened my door.

Guess it was meant to be.

Riley and her boyfriend Nate were sitting literally on top of each other in my mom's loveseat, while her two friends Alyssa and Ashley sat on the sofa next to me rubbing Frankie's belly. I looked through the sliding glass doors opposite the couch and could see people running along the track of the school field behind the house. *Maybe I'll go for a run if Thad doesn't end up wanting to hang out.*

"Tell them how you..." my sister began, throwing her arm around her boyfriend.

I connected my iPod to the stereo system next to the sofa. *Hmm. ATB? Nah. Tiësto? Not today. Ah, Paul Van Dyk.*

"Étienne!"

"What?" I looked up at my sister.

"Did you not hear a thing I said?" She shook her head, her long brown curls falling off her shoulder.

"Oh. Sorry." I shrugged, pointing to the stereo.

I know. It was probably rude of me to not pay attention to the story. Sometimes I'd turn my ears off when I had no interest in the conversation. It's hard for me to focus when I'm not interested. People used to think I was a good listener, and I thought I was. But my mind often goes off to another world once I realize what you're telling me isn't so interesting.

"You listen to this kind of stuff?" Nate grinned as he sat up and pointed to my iPod before adding, "Who is this?"

I looked up, analyzing my sister's boyfriend sitting in my mom's loveseat, legs inappropriately spread out like most straight guys sit. He wasn't a bad-looking guy, but he had this disheveled dirty-blond mop on his head, and a smirk on his face. The kind of smirk an older brother would tell his little sister to stay away from. Which I probably should have done when she first introduced me to him.

"It's Paul Van Dyk," I said.

"Who?" asked Alyssa, my sister's scrawny and frail lifelong friend.

"Paul Van Dyk. Only the best trance music DJ in existence," I replied.

"Never heard of him," said Ashley, flipping her hair off her shoulder.

The three of them asked more questions about him and his music. My sister sat there on the arm of the loveseat she and Nate occupied, and grinned as she noticed I was visibly becoming aggravated that none of them knew Paul Van Dyk. I introduced Riley to this music about a year earlier. She knew everything I knew, yet she wanted me to tell her friends instead of doing it herself.

It really was great music. Sometimes I'd lie out on the grass at night and stare up at the sky as I listened to his music on the highest volume my ears could manage. It really made me feel alive during a time when I felt empty inside.

"He's coming to perform downtown in September. I'm going to try to see if I can get a fake ID to get into the club," I explained before increasing the volume.

As the music started and my thoughts began to melt away, I looked up at the ceiling and grimaced at the small ugly popcorn-looking dots on the surface, then down to the wood paneling on the walls, and finally to the old, discolored carpet I guess was once periwinkle. *Who designed this place?* I wondered. Nothing looked right in this family room. At least not to me.

"So, Riley tells me you're a swimmer and a runner," Nate said, breaking the music's peaceful ambiance.

I nodded, pointing at the stereo with my eyes—we weren't done listening. That's one thing I hate, being interrupted while listening to music.

"Swimming? That's kind of gay," said Alyssa.

My heart sank as I turned and looked at her in disgust.

"Oh, shut up Alyssa. No, it's not," my sister interjected as she saw the rage in my eyes.

"Well, it kind of is." Nate smirked. That ugly, smartass smirk little sisters should stay away from.

"Hold it there, leotard," I yelled, reaching for the stereo, my eyes darting toward Nate. A cloud of resentment and rage forced itself through my lungs. "Who are you to call swimming gay?"

"Well, look at the tiny swimsuits." He laughed, looking at Alyssa as she also giggled. Ashley sat there looking down, knowing what was about to come.

"Yeah, so. We wear Speedos. But it's a non-contact sport. We swim in separate lanes. What are you, a wrestler? You're literally wearing a skintight outfit with a cup covering your crotch. You're on the floor with your legs and arms wrapped around another guy. Swimming. Gay? I beg to differ."

How dare they call me gay. I mean I know I am, but it isn't that obvious. Is it?

"Étienne's got a point." Ashley laughed, looking in my direction as Frankie rolled upright and climbed over her to get to me.

He could tell I was upset. And as Frankie nudged my arm, I remembered that I'd forgotten something.

5

BUTTERFLIES

S*hit. What if Thad responded and now thinks I'm ignoring him?* My phone wasn't in my pocket. I disconnected my iPod from the stereo and ran to my room.

Thad's text was waiting for me. *Haha. That's okay. What are you up to?*

What am I up to? *Should I text him back right now and say I'm free? Or should I lie and say I'm busy so I can postpone meeting him?* My fingers hovered over the keyboard.

Not much, I typed. *Just hanging out with my dog at home.*

I reluctantly clicked send and set my phone and iPod on the bed to change into something cooler since it was supposed to be an eighty-five-degree day. I hated the heat and having to wear less clothing. I wouldn't say I had a bad body, but being uncovered never felt right—again, the exception being swimming. A perfect outfit for me would be a pair of dark fitted jeans, a dark gray polo buttoned to the top, and a long-knit cardigan. I fit perfectly in the month of October, the best time of the year.

After changing, I threw on my shoes and ran to the bathroom to check on my hair. *Ugh, this humidity.* I grabbed my hair wax to try to push my stubborn hair to the side, but it did what it wanted to do. Just before I could wash the gunk off my hands, my phone started ringing.

"Argh. I'm coming," I yelled across the hall to my room, as if the person calling my phone could hear me.

I rinsed my hands off and ran to grab my phone. My heart sank into the pits of my stomach. It was Thad. Thad was calling me. Why would he be calling? Why not text?

I lifted the phone to my ear, trying not to get it wet. "Uhh, hi?"

"Hey, what's up?" His soft voice cracked.

"Umm, not much. What are you up to?" I stuttered.

"Driving around. Want to hang out? Maybe go to a café?"

Go to a café? Who is this guy? I pulled my phone back and looked at the screen in confusion. "Uh, sure. What time?" I could feel my throat shaking as I responded.

"How about now?" he responded before adding, "I'm already driving."

"Uh, yeah. Okay. Just give me a few minutes to put some clothes on." Freaking word vomit. *What is wrong with you, Étienne? You're already dressed, you idiot.*

There I was, about to die of embarrassment after declaring to him that I hadn't any clothes on. You're probably dying of secondhand embarrassment. Aren't you?

"Here, let me text you my address," I said before he could respond to my mishap.

"It's okay. I remember where you live."

You remember where I live?

Then he added, "I dropped you off there yesterday, duhh."

Okay. But I don't remember telling you where I lived yesterday either. You drove me here.

He texted *Here* a few minutes later as I frantically tried to make sure I looked presentable. Why was I making such a fuss, though? I normally made a fuss, but why so much so over a guy who probably wasn't interested in me?

"Ahem," I murmured to my sister as she watched TV with her friends.

"What do you want, Étienne?" Riley side-eyed me, her palm up.

"What's wrong with you?" I took a step back.

"What's wrong with me? You turned off the music and stormed out of here. Ass." She rolled her eyes, increasing the TV volume to shoo me away.

"Riley." I shook my head.

She ignored me, though her friends were eyeing the both of us.

"Stop!" she yelled as I stepped in front of the TV, then threw the remote on the floor by Nate's feet. "*What*, Étienne?"

"Riley. Can you let Frankie out in a little? I'm leaving. And I probably won't be back for a while."

"Gah. Leaving where?" she asked, raising her left eyebrow before adding, "I didn't hear Dana's car pull up."

"Uh. Nowhere. Can you let him out please?"

"Fine."

"I'll close the gate right now, so you don't have to worry about it," I said as I crossed the room and neared the side door.

"Whatever. Leave," she said. Ashley waved in my direction as I closed the side door.

I walked the five feet from the side door to the green metal gate and looked to my right and down the driveway. Thad was parked in the street, blocking the entrance to the driveway, and he waved when he saw me, his smile shining through the window. His straight, silvery blond hair hung over his pale-white forehead so perfectly you'd think he styled it on purpose. Maybe he did. Maybe I wasn't the only guy in school who cared about their hair.

His entire being was the complete antithesis of mine. Me with my tanned olive skin and curly brown locks, parted on the left to drape the right side of my face, and him with his relaxed hair, and skin so pale it almost looked pink.

What's he doing? I wondered as I approached the passenger door. He awkwardly leaned over the center console to open the door for me from the inside, as if my hands were full. But they weren't. It would have been weird if he got out of the car and opened the door, but this was even more awkward.

"Hey Étienne. I, um… I wasn't sure if you'd be able to get it. The door was being weird this morning," he said.

Was he as nervous as I was?

"Thanks." I smiled. But the door swung shut with ease. "So. Uh, where to?"

"Well, there's a coffee shop a couple miles down Mack. Want to go there?"

"Sure. Do they have outdoor seating?" I asked, trying to think of something to start a conversation.

"Yeah, they do. But hopefully there's an umbrella on the table or something. I'll burn to a crisp." He laughed awkwardly, then backed out of the driveway.

Yeah, you would fry in the sun. I looked down and grinned from the thought of him having to run away from the sun on a cloudless summer day.

As I looked back at the red-bricked ranch I called home, my sister's eyes caught mine. She and Nate had been peeking out from behind the curtains of the dining room, seeing this entire interaction with Thad.

Ugh. Well, there goes my cover.

At the café I ordered a lemon iced tea. It was far too hot outside to even think of drinking anything above room temperature. And I never liked coffee anyway, so it was an easy choice. Thad ordered a cappuccino. How his insides weren't melting from the scalding hot drink on a summer day beat me, but he seemed to enjoy sipping it after we found a small bench in a shaded corner on the patio facing the avenue. All of the tables shaded by parasols had already been taken.

The funny thing is, he didn't look like the kind of person who'd sip on a cappuccino at a café with someone like me. Or with anyone. He wasn't a jock, but he did stand out in a café culture setting. Was I being judgmental and stereotyping him? Maybe.

He took another sip of his drink and carefully placed the cup on its plate balancing on his bare knees. "So. What do you like to do?"

Really? What do I like to do? My eyes twitched. I was looking at the cars passing by, trying to think of how to relax myself and suppress this tight bubble of anxiety surrounding me. "I like to read and write, I guess. But I haven't done much of that in a while."

Before he could reply, I noticed he had finished his cappuccino. "Oh. How was that?" I pointed to his froth-lined cup, trying to fill the void after my short response.

"It was great. I needed a pick-me-up."

You needed a pick-me-up? Am I boring you?

"Writing? That's cool. What do you write about?" he asked, leaning against the wall to straighten his back.

"Nothing special. I write little stories here and there. I like science fiction and fantasy." I hesitated as he raised his eyebrow. "I know. Really nerdy."

"No. It's interesting." He stopped for a second and analyzed me. "Is it hard to think of things? To make up stories?"

"Not really. I daydream *a lot.*" I crossed my legs, then added, "So, it just comes to me."

"You'll have to show me some time." He smiled, forcing a tingling feeling in my stomach.

Is he serious right now? This has to be a joke. What is going on with me?

"You into any sports?" he asked.

"Kind of. I swim, and run cross country and track, but when the seasons are over, I don't really do anything."

"Oh yeah. You mentioned cross country yesterday," he replied, and I nodded with a half grin before leaning forward.

We both watched the cars driving down the avenue. The tree branches reaching over from the median swayed with the light breeze even when there weren't any cars passing by.

"I play hockey," he said after a minute of silence.

Nice one, Étienne. I probably should have asked him what he liked to do. I end up getting so taken away with answering questions about myself that I forget to ask about other people in return. I think sometimes it comes off as disingenuous.

"Hockey?" I asked, though I already knew from seeing him in his hockey jersey a few times in class over the years. "That's intense."

"Not really. I mean yeah, it can be. But I like it." He grinned.

It was funny, he didn't really look like the super muscular type you'd think of as a hockey player. I mean, he was in shape, but not intense sports kind of shape.

"Want another coffee?" I pointed to the empty cup still balanced between his two bare knees. I had finished my iced tea.

"Not really."

"Oh. Well. You ready to go then?" I added before he could continue. I don't know why I was letting my anxiety take over. We had no reason to rush.

"Well. Uh, not really. Want to walk down the avenue a little?" He gestured toward the sidewalk.

You want to spend more time with me? The thought of him still wanting to hang out with me alleviated some of my doubts. Maybe there wasn't an ulterior motive to this whole thing.

"Alrighty." My voice cracked nervously.

Thad guided us out of the café, and we headed north on Mack Avenue. I always forgot how pretty this area was with all of its little mom and pop shops. It's so much more intimate than the mammoth industrial-looking stores whose ugly parking lots took up blocks of what could have been greenery.

Thad and I sauntered for what felt like an hour, given the short distance we actually covered. He asked about my family and if I had any siblings, trying to progress our conversation from the café, but I only gave him a brief overview. He told me about his older sister, which I already knew about. She went to our school; she was only a year older than us and possessed the same physical features as her brother. Am I a creep for having noticed that?

Talking with him didn't hit the same nerves as it did whenever I had to speak to a male classmate at school. *Maybe he is genuinely interested in who I am.* Would that be the first time? Possibly. But why the sudden change?

"Oh. Do you mind if I run in for a sec?" I asked as we neared a cute pet food shop.

"Sure. I'll come too." He opened the door for me.

"Oh. Thanks." I entered.

The entrance to the first aisle was littered with every type of dog bone imaginable, and a cute, large rabbit which I guessed was the store's pet and honorary mascot. After petting the rabbit and grabbing a bag of minty veggie dog bones hanging from the wall, I looked in both directions. *Where'd he go?* I hadn't heard any steps following me and noticed I stood alone in the aisle.

"Does your dog have bad breath?" Thad laughed as he appeared from the other end of the aisle, almost making me jump.

"I mean. Not really. But clean teeth and minty breath wouldn't hurt."

He revealed a squeaker toy and squeezed it. "I'm getting this."

"You have a dog?" I raised my right brow. He hadn't mentioned it.

His eyes met mine. "No. It's for yours."

"You don't have to do that."

"I know." He turned away.

What is this? Why was he being so nice to me? I looked over as he approached the cashier to check out. But I wasn't sure what to do. I knew I wanted to get the bag of bones for Frankie. But I stood there, watching him interact with the girl behind the register. *I don't remember you being this animated in class.*

After we left the pet shop, Thad walked at such a relaxed pace that I had to force my legs to slow down. I have always been a fast walker. I walk with determination. I'm also one of those weirdos who looks everywhere while walking. I always want to see everything around me, and spot anyone I potentially know before they notice me.

"Hey. What time do you need to be home?" he asked as we neared his parked car.

"I don't know. I don't have to work today." I hesitated before adding, "I don't think it matters." *Ask me to hang out some more*, I hoped.

His eyes met mine. "I have an idea. If you have the time." He pointed to his car. I nodded.

Thad drove us south down the avenue, then turned left onto Cadieux heading toward Jefferson, the street bordering the lake and the entrance to the Detroit River.

I sat in silence, watching him from the corner of my eye. I found it strange to be driving without music. But it was okay. His presence rendered no need for background music. Like when Dana and I drove together. For the first time in the few short hours we had really known each other, the brick wall I carefully built around me started to fade. His existence in my immediate vicinity was no longer threatening. Instead, I found it somewhat comforting.

Maybe you can be my friend.

Within ten minutes, we were nearing the downtown area of Detroit. To the left of us, the arches of the Belle Isle bridge stretched over the choppy blue waters of the Detroit River. Thad merged into the turnaround lane—we were heading toward the bridge.

Thad threw his arm out in front of me and pulled open the glove compartment to grab his sunglasses, nearly giving me a heart attack when he reached in my direction.

We joined the masses in entering the island that hot summer day, then Thad turned left down a small pathway into a wooded area, far from the sunbathers and picnickers scattered along the beaches. He parked the car on the side of a dirt path, behind a tree so another car could get through comfortably. "Come on." He opened his door.

"Where are we going?" I asked. He didn't answer.

We followed the path through thick vegetation for the length of a football field until reaching a small opening, beyond which I saw a patch of clean leveled grass. *There's no way someone came through those woods to mow this one patch.*

Thad guided me across the manicured chunk of ground to sit against the thick base of an old tree. "Look at that. Sunny and shady at the same time," he said, pulling down his sunglasses. His icy blue eyes met mine.

Wow. Like looking into the bottom part of an iceberg. I knew what color his eyes were, but never had the chance to *really* look into them.

Our gazing eyes latched onto each other longer than what would be considered appropriate. Well, appropriate for two guys who were friends, one presumably being heterosexual. He wasn't just looking at me but *through* me. Like he somehow knew me and had known me for a long time. We *had* known of each other for a long time, though, hadn't we? Since childhood, really. Had he been observing me from afar all these years the way I had him? Was I finally not invisible to this person whom I wanted to know for so long? Or was I never actually invisible to him?

We sat against the trunk of the tree in silence, staring up through the shifting leaves and branches at the clear blue sky. My thoughts faded into nothing. And looking at his blank stare, I guess he felt the same. A light breeze from the river passed through the woods, giving me goose bumps as my body became one with the ground.

It was funny. I felt so comfortable and relaxed, considering my shorts and the bottom part of my shirt were probably soiled with dirt. I loved sitting on the ground, but would rather sit on a clean patch of grass or pavement. I'm fussy when it comes to the cleanliness of my clothes. But I didn't care. And I don't think he cared either.

How can silence feel so good? I asked myself, thinking about how Dana loved to hang out in the absence of noise. This felt different, though.

He had somehow flattened himself on the ground without my noticing it, so I shimmied myself down further. I felt a light pressure against my right thigh as my shorts bunched up. It was my iPod. I forgot I'd grabbed it with my phone after changing my clothes. I pulled it out and placed the iPod on my crotch so I could reposition my shorts.

"Hey. Got some good music?" Thad asked, pointing to the iPod.

"Um. Depends on how you define good," I replied.

He giggled, turning in my direction to peek through the exposed side of his shades. He reached out for one of the headphones hanging from the upper part of my left leg, and my heart pulsated violently as I scrolled through music to find something not too trancey, but still me. I wasn't sure if he'd like my taste in music.

I scooted down a little further after finding an album that I thought perfectly represented me: *Seven Years: 1998–2005*.

"Who is this?" he whispered, extending his arm behind him to rest his head.

"It's ATB. Is it okay?"

He nodded.

I had unintentionally shifted myself closer to him when I repositioned. So close that the little hairs on our upper arms could nearly kiss.

We settled there, motionless for nearly the entire album as we admired the distant passing birds in the sky above. Not a word escaped our mouths. I was content with never leaving this place, and I hoped he felt the same. He shifted his body, coming even closer to me, the warm skin of his upper arm pressing up against mine. I don't know if it was intentional, but I wouldn't have minded if it were.

Is this what it feels like to belong?

SATURDAY 07 JUNE 2008

6

ROLLER COASTER

T had had to take me back. My mom called as we neared the last few songs of the album, demanding that I come home and watch my brothers while she and my grandma ran a few errands.

"Tomorrow?" His voice cracked as he pulled up to my curb.

"I work late tomorrow. I'm sorry." I was sorry. For the first time in my life, I wanted to be around a guy.

"Saturday then?"

"How about Sunday?" I suggested. "I'm going to Cedar Point with my friend Dana and a couple other people on Saturday. We planned it like forever ago."

"Yeah. Sunday then." He smirked.

Luckily, I was able to avoid my sister for the rest of the day after our time on Belle Isle. But Friday worried me. She and I had breakfast together in the morning before I finished my chores and left for work, which made me feel uneasy since she gave me *the eye* several times as we passed each other. I knew she saw me get into Thad's car. And she knew I saw her. I suspected she was waiting for the right moment to bring it up. She loved me, but like a true little sister, she was preparing to catch me off guard. She would bombard me when she had the upper hand. That's what little sisters do. They're much more clever than little brothers.

Saturday morning came and I was fairly excited. Dana texted me early to make sure I was awake. She would pick up Samantha and Kayla first before coming to grab me, giving me time to get ready and not have to rush myself. We needed to get a head start and arrive at the park before they opened in order to get on the good coasters first. It was supposed to be a beautiful day out, which we knew would mean hours-long lines for each ride.

Of all my friends, or at least the people who sat with me during lunch, Samantha and Kayla were the only ones Dana and I actually hung out with outside of school. Though not very often on my part. The two of them were technically best friends in their own right, and they balanced each other out perfectly. Samantha got hot-headed at times and was often short-tempered, and sometimes fought with Dana. But it was warranted most of the time. Dana didn't like Samantha's boyfriend and went out of her way to make it known.

Kayla was the chill one of the group, the most levelheaded of us all, and one of the kindest people you'd ever meet. It probably helped that her parents had a lot of money and that she didn't really need to worry much about life. At least that's how it seemed.

The amusement park, Cedar Point, was about a two-hour drive on a light traffic morning. Giving us plenty of time to plan out a strategy for the day while Dana flew down I-75.

"First things first," Dana announced from the driver's seat, checking the rearview mirror. "The Millennium Force."

Samantha threw her arms up. "Dana, but that's on the other side of the park. We could hit up like two really good rides before getting there."

"Why don't we do one before the Millennium Force," said

Kayla as she flipped a page in the book she was reading. "Like the Top Thrill Dragster?"

Along with being the most levelheaded, she was also an insane bookworm. And I mean that as a sincere compliment. I'd almost never seen her without a book in hand. Once, in sixth grade, she read all of the Lord of the Rings books in less than a week. We went as friends to senior prom. Sadly, that night didn't turn out as planned. *I'm sorry for that, Kayla.*

"I think we should do that," I whispered to Dana. Obviously, I was going to agree with Kayla.

Dana rolled her eyes and shrugged, giving in to our plan.

There wasn't much traffic since it was so early in the morning, and we crossed the Ohio border with ease. I say that we crossed the border with ease due to the lack of patrol cars on the freeway. There is no real border between Michigan and Ohio, but there are always cop cars hiding in the ditches on the side of the freeway trying to catch us Michiganders driving over the speed limit. We do like to speed, especially those of us from metro-Detroit.

My phone vibrated as we neared the off ramp. *Have a nice time on the coasters*, texted Thad. Just this one message made my morning, rendering me more anxious to see him the next day.

"Hey. Did you guys see on the news that California is legalizing gay marriage?" Kayla interrupted the last part of our music-filled ride, which I was fine with since Dana was listening to hardcore punk. But why did Kayla bring this up now? *They've been talking about it for weeks now*, I thought, looking out my window.

"I didn't see that," Samantha said.

I kept quiet to observe their reactions. They were my friends and I loved them, but I really hoped they'd bring some positivity to this subject.

Dana rolled her eyes. "Whatever. I don't care. Let them get married."

"Well, they don't choose who they love, so why not?" replied Kayla.

"What do you mean they don't choose? They're not born that way," Dana spat.

My heart sank. How could my best friend think this way about me? I had only ever told one person I was gay—and I'll save that for later. But if Dana said this during the conversation in the car, this was how she really felt. Maybe it was a good thing I didn't tell her about Thad.

"Oh, come on Dana. Yes, they are. How could you choose to live a harder life and be made fun of all the time? You wouldn't. It's not a choice," Samantha insisted.

"Look. My uncle's gay. I'm totally fine with it. But because he's gay doesn't mean my brother and I are. It's not like, genetic," she replied.

Samantha raised her brows. "Dana. I think you're talking about heredity. We're not talking about that. We're talking about the fact that gay people don't choose to be gay."

"Whatever. Let them marry if they want."

I'd be lying if I said I wasn't surprised by Samantha's defense. It moved me. She was the religious person in our group. I was happy to see the way Samantha and Kayla unknowingly defended me. Yet Dana's reaction saddened me. I had never seen this side of my friend before. Yeah, she was hot-headed sometimes, but she was usually laid-back and didn't care about politics and stuff like that.

She knows me though. She has to know I'm gay. Come on, Dana.

The rest of the day felt like a blur. I went through the motions and followed the girls on all the rides. I tried my best not to bring the morale of the group down. But Kayla noticed I was mute while eating lunch.

"Étienne. You okay?" Kayla whispered as Dana and Samantha ran to buy a pop.

"I have a headache." I looked down at my barely eaten food, trying to pay attention to the screams of thrill-seekers on coasters in the distance. If I wasn't having fun, I could at least listen to other people having the time of their lives.

The fact was, I felt lost. I felt betrayed by the only person who I thought really knew me. I understood that it was a difference in opinion. But it still felt like a punch in the gut. A veil of anxiety and doubt repositioned itself over my thoughts. I had to do what I'd always done: reinforce the wall so no one could hurt me again.

The only part of the day that I really enjoyed was when I went on the Corkscrew by myself while the girls waited in line for the bathroom. Which was pretty ridiculous if you ask me. The park *did not* have enough facilities. Come on. We all know there needs to be more. Women don't have the ease of urinals like we men do, though I never use urinals. Standing there next to another guy with so little privacy freaks me out.

The Corkscrew was my favorite ride—my inner Eeyore couldn't distract me while I passed through the coaster's twists and turns. It was also my favorite because it was the first roller coaster I'd ever ridden. My dad took me on it. He hated coasters, but was afraid he wouldn't look manly if he refused the first time I asked him to take me on it.

I sat in the back with Kayla during the ride home and remained silent, staring out the window the entire way back. I knew I was probably letting my emotions get the better of me, but I was entitled to that. Was I not?

My phone dinged as Dana prepared to merge into the right lane for the next exit on I-94. *Was it busy today?* Thad's message read.

It's him! my conscience yelled. I couldn't believe how my mood transformed in an instant. How was that possible? How could someone I barely knew make me feel so much better?

It was whatever. Ended up being a shitty day. I clicked send even though I didn't really want to share my state of mind for risk of him asking me what happened.

I looked ahead through the windshield from the back seat as we exited the freeway and noticed Dana eyeing me in the rearview mirror.

"Anyone want to come over for a little while? My parents are up north. We could drink," she said, holding my gaze in the mirror.

Kayla and Samantha excitedly announced that they would *definitely* be joining Dana. But I still felt out of place. For the first time in the many years that I had known Dana, I felt uncomfortable being around her. And I didn't like it.

"Can you drop me off at home? Our third round on the Millennium Force messed with my stomach," I lied. I honestly wanted to go home, flatten my body on the bed in silence with Frankie, and stare up at the ceiling as I listened to music. *The twins better not be bothering him*, I hoped.

I caught Dana's eye again in the mirror as she pulled up into the driveway. "Thanks for driving, Dana." I sighed and waved goodbye to Kayla and Samantha as the door slammed.

Why are all the lights on? I asked myself while opening the gate. *Mom's probably not home.* My siblings usually liked to flip all the switches on when they were alone.

"Hey."

I turned and closed the gate behind me. It was Riley.

"Why are all the lights on?" I demanded. "Where's Ma?"

"My *god*. Already in a mood," she replied.

"Ehh, sorry. I don't feel well."

"I got back from Nate's. She took Callum and Niall to Grandma's for dinner. They've been there for a while I guess," she said, then squinted behind me as we heard the bang of a car door.

"Hey Riley," Dana said.

I sighed. *What does Dana want? Go home.*

"Dana," my sister said, pushing me to the side to reopen the gate and embrace my friend.

"Étienne. Are you sure you don't want to come hang out for a while? There's something on your mind. I know you," she said, fixing her orange ponytail.

No, you don't. Not anymore. I shrugged, then started toward the side door.

"Come on, Étienne. What the hell happened? Everything was fine this morning until we got there," she said.

My sister looked back and forth from Dana to me, a mischievous grin forming on her face. "Would this have anything to do with your new friend, Étienne?"

I'm going to die, and my sister is coming with me.

Dana tilted her head as her eyes met with my sister's. A long and awkward silence stretched between us before Dana turned back to me and asked, "What friend? Is this why you're being weird lately?"

I looked at my sister, eyes wide open, trying to will a threat to her psychically. This was the moment. The moment she was waiting for. A moment when I was vulnerable, and she would have the upper hand.

"That guy who's in your grade. You know, the one with the silvery blond hair. Pretty popular. I think his name is Thad." My sister smirked, giving me the side eye.

How do you know his name? Probably that boyfriend of yours.

"What. Uh, why? Étienne, you don't even know him." Dana put her hands on her hips.

I felt both sets of eyes staring me down, trying to penetrate my skull. I glanced at my sister, wishing this could end. *Thanks a lot, Riley.*

"It's nothing." I felt my face starting to burn. *But it isn't nothing. I don't want to tell the two of you.* "We bumped into each other after school the other day and I offered to help him with something. That's it."

Dana wasn't buying it. She knew I was lying. "Fine. Whatever. That better be it then. He... I don't trust him, and you shouldn't either."

"K, Mom." I rolled my eyes and headed toward the door. "Bye." I turned my head back one last time and my eyes met Dana's. Hurt shone in her eyes, and anger. Hurt, probably in learning that her best friend was keeping something from her. But why anger?

"Riley! What was that?" I demanded once my sister entered the side door, both of us in the entrance hall, our bodies reflected in the mirrored sliding doors of the coat closet.

"What was what? You *are* being weird lately."

"Seriously, Riley? You know Dana snaps quickly. Why would you bring that up? I don't talk about what you do with your friends."

"Oh really?" she snapped, her hand resting on her hip. "Look how rude you were to Nate the other day."

"What? I wasn't rude. He's annoying with his ugly smirk and ridiculous hair. And your friends probably think so too."

"Whatever, Étienne." She rolled her eyes and began to turn away, toward the rear living room.

"Just leave me alone, Riley!"

7

HOUSE PARTY?

"What a bitch," I said to myself as I grabbed Frankie from the sofa and carried him to my room, slamming the door behind me. Why would my sister do this to me? Why wouldn't she just ask me about it? She and I usually had each other's back. I felt betrayed by my sister, the only person in this family who had never tried getting in my way. We had an unspoken pact. A code. We got along. I stayed out of her way and kept the secrets she didn't want people to know, and she respected my space and privacy.

And what have I done to you, Dana? I thought bitterly. *Really though, what had I done to her to warrant such a warning and sour response?*

Frankie curled up to my leg after I threw myself on the floor. I was leaning on the side of my bed, my eyes closed, trying to push away the unsavory thoughts that flooded my mind. I sat there for several minutes, ignoring the sounds of my twin brothers and my mom returning from my grandma's house. I then felt a tap on my thigh. Frankie had turned over onto his back, his left paw reaching over to me, begging to give him a belly rub.

"Mister Frankie want some rubs," I blurted as he turned toward me, forcing the skin on his head to tighten, revealing the whites of his eyes. I reached down to scratch the outsides of his hind legs, and he elongated his already long and stout body. *You always know just what I need, little man.*

I leaned down to give him a peck on the nose, triggering him to gently lick his left nostril. It's funny how dogs always lick their noses after a kiss. I grabbed my iPod from the bedside drawer, but a sudden vibration from my pocket stopped me.

Sorry to hear that. You okay? he texted.

I gasped, forgetting that I had texted him before returning home from Cedar Point.

Yeah, I'm fine. Thanks for asking. Nothing some time with my dog won't fix. But really, was I fine?

The time spent with Frankie made me feel better. It was relaxing. But thoughts of Dana still swirled around in the back of my mind. On one hand I wanted to distance myself from her after the comments in the car and the warning she gave me about Thad. On the other, I couldn't imagine a life without my childhood best friend.

Haha. My phone vibrated again before he added, *You up for anything tonight?*

"Am I up for anything tonight?" I whispered. *I'm a seventeen-year-old gay kid with barely any friends and no car*, I thought. *Why wouldn't I be?*

Nothing planned. You? I replied. He was asking, so maybe he wanted something to happen.

Going to my cousin's house party across town, want to come? He responded so quickly I could only infer that he *did* want me to come.

"A house party," I read out loud as Frankie nudged my leg again for more attention. I'd never been to a house party before. Not once. I didn't think people saw me as the house party type of person. Dana and even some of our other friends had thrown house parties throughout sophomore and junior year, but they never invited me. I always had to learn about it Monday mornings as they gossiped about who puked where and who slept with who. I usually pretended it didn't bother me, but it did. Why hadn't they ever invited me? *Maybe I should go.* Wouldn't you?

Yeah. I'd like that, I typed out, grinning.

He immediately texted back. *Cool. Be there in 15.*

I jumped up, scaring Frankie half to death, causing him to roll over. "Sorry, little man."

I threw on my favorite dark navy jeans and my nicer shoes, then grabbed a charcoal gray polo from my top drawer before sneaking out of my room and heading to the bathroom. Luckily no one heard me, and after a few minutes of fidgeting with my clothes and my hair, I snuck back into my room to grab my phone, wallet, and keys. "Should I bring my iPod?" I asked myself. *Yes. You never know.*

My pockets were stuffed with all of my important belongings: wallet in the back-left pocket and phone in the right; keys in the front left pocket and iPod in the right. I glanced in the mirror before leaving my room to make sure I didn't look like a clown with pudgy pockets, then grabbed a cardigan before discreetly closing my door. You never know when it's going to be cold in Michigan. Always be prepared for our bipolar weather.

I texted Thad to meet me in front of the stop sign a few houses down. I didn't want to chance Riley catching me again and causing more unrest.

"What?" I looked a few houses down, wondering why he was outside of his car, leaning against the stop sign.

"Why are you dressed up? It's not that kind of a party." He giggled.

You didn't have to get out of your car.

I looked down at what I was wearing. "This isn't dressed up. It's comfortable."

"Comfortable?" He raised his brow, looking down at my shoes, then up at my neck.

"Huh." I took a deep breath when he lifted his hand toward my chest, then loosened my polo by undoing the top button. My stomach jumped and my fists clenched.

How bold, I thought as his eyes met mine. Who gave him permission to cross over my personal space like that? Normally I try to avoid unwarranted physical touch, especially when people want to touch my face or hair. Even now people try to touch my hair. *"Who does your hair?"* they ask as I lean back to avoid their contact. I know my hair looks nice, but please don't touch it. It takes time and effort for me to style it. The funny thing is, I didn't squirm or move away when he neared me.

"There. Less uptight." He smirked.

"Uptight? I'm not uptight. I like the way a structured, buttoned-up polo looks around my neck." I grabbed my collar bone area.

"Um. Okay." Trying to hold in a laugh, he signaled me to get in the car.

The drive there felt very much like our drive to Belle Isle. No music. No speaking. No sound. Just the two of us enjoying each other's company, Thad yelling out "Ope" whenever he needed to swerve around a dreaded Michigan pothole. And as we ventured further into the northern suburbs, the houses began to look more and more alike. The lack of trees was unfortunate. In our area tall, old trees littered every street, towering over everything and giving everyone's yard much-needed shade during the summer. And providing days' worth of fun jumping into piles of leaves in the autumn.

The house party was an actual house party, which blew me away since the few photos I'd seen of my friends' parties only looked like medium-size gatherings. His cousin lived in a big house out where newer subdivisions were being built. People lingered in every room on the first floor and in the basement. Every flat surface imaginable was covered in a pyramid of half-empty plastic cups and empty bottles and cans. The ceiling of nearly every room featured a built-in surround sound stereo system. You couldn't hear yourself think.

I roamed the house with some sort of potent punch in my hand, then decided to sit on a small chair in the corner of the living room after losing Thad to his cousin. I sat there for a little while sipping on my drink, taking it all in. "People really do this kind of stuff?" I whispered to myself while watching a couple on the other side of the room make out, knocking over their drinks onto the rug. I couldn't believe I was part of something like this. And even though I knew no one at the party except for Thad, I was happy that for once I wasn't left out. For the first time, someone thought to include me in something fun, an experience no one should miss.

Where is he? After finishing my drink, I got up to go find him. I was feeling a little funny from the alcohol and started to worry how I'd get home if he left me there.

Hey. Still here? I messaged him, trying to step over a guy who clearly had too much to drink and was crawling on all fours, blocking the hallway between the living room and the kitchen.

I thought I saw him from the corner of my eye before nearing the kitchen but was interrupted by a tap on my shoulder. I turned, and a girl I'd never met before grabbed my left hand, then shoved a shot glass in my right. She encouraged me to down it in one gulp—which I did—then dragged me through the hallway to the small library at the back of the house. Well, it wasn't as much a library as an office with a few bookcases. A few chairs and a sofa filled with older people I didn't know lined the room. A makeshift bar sat on the computer table. This girl, who I'm certain was a couple years older than me, poured another two shots and demanded that I take one. I obliged. Why? I wasn't sure. Would you have obliged?

After a second shot of what I remember being whisky, I squeezed myself into the corner of the couch with the others. The unnamed girl handed me a beer and lay across the laps of the people next to me, resting her head in my lap. This was new, and it was fun. But a sense of uncertainty cloaked my vision as I remembered that I needed to find Thad. He was my safe space in this strange house.

The girl grabbed my face, directing my gaze toward her, then winked. *What is going on? I have to get out of here.* My stomach began to churn, and I leaned back, trying to sink into the couch. She lifted herself up and tried to pull me closer to her, inching her face nearer to meet mine.

I CANNOT do this! Panic began to engulf my being.

"No. I need to get up." I wormed myself up and over the armrest, falling to the side of the couch and spilling beer all over my legs. I jumped up and took a chug of the remaining foamy liquid, then set the bottle on the floor and left the room.

The ceiling started to drop in on me and people around me were spinning. I'd consumed too much alcohol. "Need some air," I whispered, then beelined to the kitchen and nearly fell through the back door. I stopped for a minute on the back patio, trying to hold in the burning, sickening feeling in my stomach. I took a deep breath to try to push down whatever was coming up and headed over to the tree in the back corner of the yard.

I threw myself to the ground on the side of the tree that faced the bushes to the back of the yard so no one could see me and propped myself up against the trunk. I couldn't lie down and let my blurred vision take control. I couldn't move another muscle without triggering a reaction from my flaming insides. "This is not fun. I'm never drinking like this again," I mumbled.

My phone hadn't vibrated since I last texted Thad, so I closed my eyes and took deep breaths to alleviate my motionless motion sickness. I unintentionally fell asleep for a while. At least that's what I think happened.

Two strong hands cupped my shoulders. "Étienne. Hey. You okay?"

Oh good. You didn't leave me.

SUNDAY 08 JUNE 2008

8

MORNING AFTER

"Come on. Let's get you some water," he said into my ear.

Thad helped me up from the base of the tree and pulled my arm over him. It was still dark out, which meant I hadn't been asleep for too long. And people were still inside drinking, though many had left. Thad brought me into the kitchen where I leaned up against the island to keep my balance while inhaling a glass of water.

"Thank you," I coughed after accidentally breathing in some water. "Are we leaving?"

"Leaving? You're in no shape to be riding over Michigan potholes. And I drank a lot." He pointed to the beer he was still sipping, then gave me a wink.

What happened? I wondered. *Why did he wink at me? Was that a flirtatious wink? Or was he also drunk and joking around?*

He refilled my glass of water as I was feeling through my pockets to make sure I didn't drop anything anywhere. The headphones attached to my iPod were tangled, so I pulled them out and put them on the countertop to try to unknot them.

"You brought your iPod?" He raised his eyebrow.

"I, uhm..."

"Hey, I have an idea." He grabbed my arm and wrapped it over his shoulder.

I'm fine now. I can walk. But I let him hold on to me anyway as we slid through the crowd and ascended the stairs to the second floor. He guided me to the right, and we entered what looked like a spare bedroom with a sliding door that led to a small balcony.

"Want to listen to that album you showed me the other day? What's the DJ's name, ABT?"

"ATB. Yeah. We almost finished it. There was only like one song left," I replied, hoping he would set me down somewhere.

"Why not start from the beginning?" he suggested as he slid open the balcony door, still holding on to me.

Two beanbags filled up almost the entirety of the balcony. Thad sat on the green one and I sank into the blue, my favorite color. My body felt too heavy to scooch over, and I didn't think the headphone wire would reach him. Which he eventually noticed. He saw me struggling to untangle the wire again and decided to reposition himself so that he was lying down, head rested on my beanbag close to my left ear. He reached out and grabbed the headphones from me, then handed me one of the ears after untangling them.

"Thanks," I looked up toward him, my left eye nearly touching his right brow.

"You're a pretty cool guy, Étienne," he said before I was about to click play, my stomach fluttering more than it ever had.

I rested my thumb on the iPod to let the silence of the outdoors consume us for a minute. *I'm a cool guy?* Thinking again of what he declared sent another round of butterflies through my stomach. Not anxious butterflies. Real ones. The *I like you* tingling feeling.

"I think you're cooler," I whispered, then restarted the album.

We lay there staring up at the moon's remaining half,

continuing our quest to listen to and finish the album together. We were both immobile, the night sky absorbing us, lying silently in intoxication—not just intoxicated from the amount of alcohol running through our veins, but also, at least for me, drunkenly happy to have created a friendship in such short time. He thought I was cool, which I'd never heard anyone say before about me. And I felt the same about him. Well, maybe more.

I've realized how much I like you. I wonder if you feel the same? I thought, my gaze still fixated on the moon. *If not, it's all right. As long as we're friends.*

The ringing of my phone woke me. We had fallen asleep. It was morning, and the sky was bright. *Damn. It's Mom.* I pulled the phone out of my pocket and rubbed my dry eyes to let my vision and contact lenses focus. Sleeping with contact lenses on is not a good idea. I rejected the call.

"Shit, gotta think of where I was last night," I whispered.

A text from my mom came through. *I thought you were home when I came in last night? Étienne, where are you? Answer your phone.*

Someone was touching me, I realized. I turned my head and there he was. Thad. He must have repositioned his body during the night. He lay parallel to me, his arm around my stomach. How did this happen? Were we really that drunk? We were fully clothed, which meant nothing had happened, not that anything would have. I was amazed that he didn't wake up and push himself off me. This was innocent. We were drunk and listening to music, then fell asleep. That was it.

My iPod had settled on the beanbag, nearly hidden under the lower part of his shirt. *What the...* I looked a little further down and there it was, plain as day. He was sleeping with his arm around me—and he was hard. It was outlined through his jeans against his inner thigh. I looked around to make sure nobody was watching us, then looked back down at him.

He stirred, starting to wake. I looked away and pretended I was still asleep.

"Argh. What?" He promptly pulled his arm from my side, rolling to get up. "Shit. Shit. What time is it?" he whispered, the fear revealing itself through his cracking voice.

He was panicking. He didn't expect to be here. I'm sure as hell he didn't expect to find his arm around me either. He was probably mortified feeling himself nearly pressed up against me.

Thad stood there behind me quietly for a moment. I wasn't sure what he was doing. Maybe he was admiring me. Or maybe not. He was probably frozen, horrified that he fell asleep so close to another guy. A guy he had been classmates with, but hadn't really known until not even a week prior. He stood there for a few minutes, then softly slid the glass door open and stepped inside. He left the door open, probably not to wake me.

I was content with how the night went, even if that meant being grounded when I got home. *Yeah. Like Mom's gonna ground me.*

I lay there for a few more minutes and understood he was most likely not coming back. He was probably brimming with fear and anxiety. I decided to push myself out of the squishy beanbag.

"Hey," I heard as I bent over to grab my iPod from between the two massive beanbags. He stood awkwardly in the doorway, his cheeks reddening, his hands submerged deep into his front pockets.

"Hey. I didn't mean to fall asleep. Did I keep you from going home?" I asked, trying to pretend that I didn't know he lay next to me the whole night.

"No. It's all right. My parents knew I was here." He shrugged, then pulled out his hand and scratched the back of his head. He looked flustered.

My head started to throb as I entered the spare bedroom. "Argh. Wow, that's insane." I grabbed the side of my head. The pulsating pain forced me to close my right eye. I tried to look toward him, and he loosened up and headed toward me.

"Let's go get you something to eat." His hand rested on my lower back to guide me through the house.

Thankfully, we left his cousin's house undetected. I'm sure most of those who stayed were probably still sleeping long after we left. They stayed up drinking much later than we had.

We stopped at a small diner on the way home.

"So. That was something," I joked, stuffing maple syrup-soaked pancakes into my mouth.

"It was." He grinned, looking down, forking his scrambled eggs.

"I don't think I've ever had that much to drink before."

He giggled. "Yeah, I guessed that."

"Seriously? Did I embarrass myself? This girl kept shoving shots in my face. I couldn't really say no." I looked at him.

"You're fine. You held it in like a champ, considering it was your first time at a party."

Champ? Who says champ?

"Anyway," he went on, "that was my cousin's girlfriend. I saw her dragging you across the hall. You looked frightened. Like you didn't know what do to." He shook his head, laughing.

Girlfriend? Your cousin's girlfriend tried to kiss me. Not cool.

My phone dinged again. I ignored the several attempts my mom made at trying to reach me. What was I going to tell her? *Where are you?* the text message read.

Sorry just woke up. Went to Dana's after Cedar Point, I lied. I needed to figure out a way to ease her. I'd never not come home before unless I was with a cousin, and she knew about it in advance.

She tried calling again, and I ignored it.

Ma. They're still sleeping. I'm getting up. Be home soon, I texted.

My phone dinged again. *Your sister told me you were home last night.*

I sighed, frustrated. *Really, Riley? This is a new low*, I thought before writing, *Yeah. Then I walked over to Dana's later on.*

Now I was in trouble. My sister had to open her massive mouth again, didn't she? I now had to think of something to say to Mom. Something believable about where I was. Something to put her at ease so she wouldn't call Dana's parents, which would end in disaster for Dana and me.

I asked Thad to drop me off in the school parking lot to make it seem like I walked home from Dana's. My mom would have been suspicious if she saw me being dropped off by an unknown car.

He pulled into the lot and parked in the back under the thick branches of a tree hanging over the fencing. I was surprised to see a few cars in the parking lot. *It's Sunday, and it's summer. Who's here?*

"I had a fun time last night. Thanks for inviting me." My eyes caught his before I added, "And for helping navigate my drunken body back into the house."

We sat in silence for a while. He gave the impression of being content, but I could see that he was thinking about something. Was he regretting having woken up next to me? Would he continue to talk to me? I hoped he would. I really did. It had only been four days since he approached me outside on the last day of school, but I felt like we made a connection. I had a new friend. Who knew I would ever be able to make a guy friend? I sure didn't.

"Well, uhh. I'm going to go. Thanks again." I unbuckled and reached for the door handle.

"Erm. Wait a second." He looked up at me, blushing as he tapped his foot on the floor.

I took my hand off the handle and shifted to face him. He

looked to the side, then looked down, avoiding eye contact as he brought his hands together and cracked his knuckles. We sat quietly for another minute. He twisted his body toward me, lifting and then resting his exposed knee on the center console. *How can a knee look so enticing?*

His eyes eventually met with mine. I never noticed that he had such long eyelashes. They were visible in a lonely ray of dappled light.

"I, uhh. About last night," he began. "You, ahh, didn't happen to wake up while I was still there?"

I knew this was coming. I hoped he wasn't upset about it. "I did. It's fine. Don't worry about it." I waved my hand. I didn't want to lie to him. I could have continued to pretend that I was asleep, but I'd rather this new friendship start off with honesty. At least on my part.

He looked down, awkwardly holding his hands together before looking me in the eye again. "Thank you. I didn't expect that."

Didn't expect what? To have your arm around me? Or to have a hard-on while your arm was around me?

Maybe he didn't feel anything for me. It could have been normal morning wood. *There's no reason to fret about that. We all get it.*

"Well. I need to head out before my mom sends a search party after me," I joked.

"Étienne," I heard him yell after I closed the door, rolling down the window as I started walking away. "Thanks," he said after I turned to look at him.

I watched as he left the parking lot, then turned toward the alley behind the school where the fencing bordered my street. I jumped the fence to my backyard. Taking the long way home like I had planned no longer interested me.

"Ton— Ugh. Étienne. Where were you last night?" Mom demanded, banging on my bedroom door.

My mom was thankfully in the shower when I got home, but of course my twin brothers had to make a deal about me not being home that morning. And when they did, I ran to my room and made sure my door was held shut. I didn't think it a big deal. There were plenty of other teenagers who stayed over at their friends' on summer nights without telling their parents. Plus, a seventeen-year-old is nearly an adult. Right?

"Hold on, Ma. I'm going to take a shower," I said as I banged my side of the door.

"What did you just...? Get your ass out here now. You can take a shower later."

You've got to be kidding me.

I threw on some clean clothes so my mom wouldn't detect the smell of beer on my jeans. I then ran to the bathroom and gargled some mouthwash to mask my breath.

She was waiting for me in the rear living room. And before I even entered, she began with a lecture about responsibility and communication. And how even though I was practically an adult, I still needed to let her know what was going on.

"Get outta here!" she scolded my spying twin brothers. But only Niall visibly exited the room.

"Look. I trust you, Étienne. More than I trust any of them." She gestured where Callum was obviously hiding with his walkie talkie. "But you need to tell me where you're going. You can't disappear like that."

"Okay. All right," I said, promising that I would let her know when I was going to be out.

"Étienne." She leaned in closer to me and lowered her voice to hide the rest of the conversation from Callum. "I know you weren't at Dana's last night."

"I'm going to kill Riley." I flew out of the sofa and headed toward the sliding glass door that divided the rear living room and our yard. My sister was peacefully sunbathing on the back porch.

"Étienne. Stop. It's not her fault."

What do you mean it's not her fault? Whose fault would it be? Who else saw me with Thad the other day and then bumped into me when Dana dropped me off last night? She could have kept her mouth shut. But she didn't.

"Nobody needed to say anything, Étienne. A mom knows. I already knew. You're hiding something from me, and I don't like it."

"Ma, I'm not hiding anything. Can I go now?"

"Don't lie. I know you better than you know yourself. What's going on with you this year? You used to tell me everything."

"Nothing. I was hanging out with a friend. That's it," I tried reassuring her.

"Who? What's his name?"

Now this was prying. "What do you mean *his* name? Nobody, Ma. I have more friends than just Dana."

She shook her head, looking down at my feet and changing her tone. "You don't need to hide from me. You can tell me anything, honey."

"It's nothing." I started to leave the room. "Going to take a shower."

Okay, yes. It was something. I was hiding from my mom. But she always made a big deal whenever I did something new with my life. I'll never forget what a fuss she made when I first started shaving my face. Or when I first started growing body hair, which I gladly got rid of thanks to being on the swim team. Or when I wanted to use my own money to purchase my own clothes after getting my first summer job after freshman year. It's like she was obsessed with me. Always Étienne this, and Étienne that. *"Étienne, can you watch the twins? Étienne, can you run some errands for me?"* she'd ask me. Then, *"Can you believe how great my son Étienne is?"* she would say to people.

She could be somewhat smothering. I love my mom, and I

wouldn't change her for the world. I knew I was hiding some-thing from her. Hiding the fact that I was changing. That I wanted new friends. That I liked someone, who probably didn't like me the same way. I was finally ready to start building my own life. Was it too much to ask for some space?

MONDAY 09 JUNE 2008

9

ICE CREAM

"**O**h my god. He fell asleep next to you?" Rhonda screeched, jumping with excitement.

I nodded, smiling after finally being able to tell someone about my weekend activities. Rhonda worked with me at the jewelry store, where I worked as an assistant. I only worked there a few days a week. It wasn't much fun since Jason, the owner and general manager, always made little comments here and there, hinting at my masculinity, or lack thereof. But it paid better than any other part-time job a high school kid could have. On the plus side, I had Rhonda. She was in her twenties, though she acted like she was sixteen when she hung out with me during our shifts. She was genuinely interested in my life and asked about my friends and family, and even tried to invite me to her girls' nights.

She was the only person at the time who knew who I was. Who knew I was different from other guys. And she didn't make a big deal about it. She let me be me.

"He did," I replied. "But he got up really fast when he realized he was lying next to me."

"So, we like him, right? Like, *liiike him?*" she asked, sipping on a mug of freshly brewed coffee, running her fingers through her hair.

"I think I do. Is that weird?" I replied. I was on the floor sorting through boxes of wax molds, and I looked up at her.

"Why would it be weird?" She raised an eyebrow.

"I guess I'm a little unsure. We started talking to each other like less than a week ago. It's weird. He's never really spoken to me before."

"It's not weird. Get out of your damn head, Étienne, and stop thinking about it. Did he seem to have a nice time the other night?" She tilted her head, wide eyed.

"Well. Yeah, I think he did. But I'm not sure if it's the same *nice time* that I had." I looked up at her towering over me. She rolled her eyes.

"Feel it out then. That's what I do with a man. Hang out with him and keep an eye out for hints. You can usually tell if a guy likes you after hanging out a few times."

"I think it's probably different in my case."

"Pff. Shut up, Étienne. All guys are the same. Even you." She winked then turned to walk back onto the floor as she saw Jason enter the back room.

All guys are the same? Not sure about that.

"On the floor again with your legs crossed, eh?" Jason rolled his eyes.

"It's easier to sort through everything on the floor. The tables aren't big enough." I stood up.

"Never mind, Étienne. You didn't get it." He waved his hand, then left the room, the ceiling light reflecting off his bald head.

But I did get it. I understood what he meant when he mentioned me being on the floor with my legs crossed. I did the same thing every time he asked me to sort through the boxes of molds. This time I decided to act oblivious. If I didn't give him the satisfaction of a negative reaction, maybe he'd stop.

Dana texted me near the end of my shift. *Hey, can we hang out?* I didn't really feel like having her over and wasn't up to walking to her house. We agreed to meet at the ice cream shop on the corner of the next block after dinner.

At the end of my shift, I hurriedly left the building before my mom had the chance to come in and say hi to everyone. *I need to get a car*, I thought.

"How was work?" my mom asked before I could reach the buckle.

"Ehh, it was fine." I shrugged. There wasn't much to talk about. And I wasn't about to bring up Jason's subtle homophobia to my mom.

She lowered the music. "You doing anything tonight?"

"Don't know. Might hang out with Dana later." I was being short, but I didn't feel like talking to any of my family members. Not after what Riley did.

"K. If you say so."

"What? Ma. You can read her text message if you want." I pointed to the phone between my legs. *Why is she being like this? I'm not lying to her. Not this time.*

My sister brought Nate over for dinner, which was a good distraction for us all. My grandma threw questions at him left and right, which tore the ugly smirk off his face, taking the attention away from everyone else. She didn't really like that my sister was dating. *"Brenda. She's too young to be dating,"* my grandma would say. She even winked at me after asking Nate what his intentions were with Riley, and why he never passed a comb through his hair. By the time she finished questioning him, it looked as if he had plunged his face into my sister's blush palette. I loved it.

It was nice being invisible again, until I wasn't.

"You next," Grandma said. "I hear you made a new friend."

A malicious smirk appeared on my sister's and Nate's faces.

"What? No." Panic started to take hold of my voice. Was this really happening?

"Who's the guy that picked you up last Thursday?" she asked.

Nate turned to my sister, who immediately looked down and bit her lip as she noticed me giving her the death stare. I was trying to figure out who this person was across the table from me. Did her boyfriend put her up to it? Or was she becoming one of those teenage mean girls?

"Oh. No one. Just someone from school." I tried to blow it off, but I think my face might have said it all. *Please stop. I don't want to talk about it.*

"Your sister didn't seem to think it was no one." She pointed at Riley.

"Okay. Uh, Étienne aren't you meeting Dana for ice cream? You should get changed; it's getting cooler out." My mom broke the tension, saving me.

Thanks Mom, I said with a look. My mom could be nosy and pushy sometimes, but she knew when enough was enough. And this was definitely not the time to be in my business.

I got up from the table then cleared my plate. My sister looked at me as I passed her, but I pretended she wasn't there. I couldn't look at her without exposing my rage. *Maybe this has something to do with me embarrassing Nate the other day.* That's what it was. I embarrassed him in front of his girlfriend and her friends. That was probably why they were spying in the first place.

"Hey Étienne. Who's this new friend?" Callum asked.

My brothers followed me to my room instead of finishing their dinner. They were unusually calm, sitting at the end of my bed as I changed into something warmer.

"Come on, Étienne. Please tell us. We won't tell," added Niall.

"Look guys. It's no one. There's this guy who goes to school with me. And he wants to be friends. That's all." I tried giving them as little detail as possible.

"Well, I think it's cool," Niall whispered, looking down as he swung his legs back and forth, shifting my bed.

"Oh yeah?" I gave him a questioning stare.

"Yeah," Callum replied. "You're always hanging out with girls. You're a guy, you should have guy friends too, not just Dana."

Niall nodded, following his counterpart.

"Well Dana's my best friend. You know that." I pointed at the two of them then added, "It's okay for boys to be friends with girls. You know that, right?"

Why were they being so agreeable? These weren't the twin brothers I was used to.

"Can we go with you for ice cream?" they asked in unison.

That's why you're both being nice.

"Why not," I replied. "But go get a sweater on or something. It's getting dark and cool out."

I don't know why I agreed to them coming. They normally aggravated me beyond reason, which was why I never really hung out with them. Fortunately, they were notably quiet and followed me as we walked to the ice cream shop.

"Callum. Niall!" Dana threw out her arms. She changed her hair yet again, this time to a fiery red.

"Sorry about them. They wanted to tag along."

Dana and I stood in line at the front window while the twins saved a picnic table for us. Well, Callum threw himself on an empty table as a family was approaching.

I no longer wanted to be bothered by what Dana had said in the car. I wanted to forget about it and just be her friend. She looked at me, biting her lower lip.

"I think I like the red better than the orange." I pointed to her hair, trying to break the ice.

"You were feeling fine the other day, weren't you? I think I know why you were so absent the whole time. Was it what I said in the car?" she murmured as we took a step closer to the order window.

"What do you mean?" I said, pretending to look at the ice cream menu hanging from the ceiling.

"Étienne. I know. Well, I've only recently figured it out. But I had to have known. It's obvious now that I think about it."

Her words pounded my stomach with the velocity of a bull running headfirst into its target. I felt like I was going to hurl. My face snapped toward her, my eyes starting to swell. I took a breath but couldn't say anything due to the pounding in my chest.

"It's okay, Étienne. I'm fine with it. I'm sorry you had to hear that." She was trying to comfort me as I felt the color slowly drain from my face. But it didn't help.

"Hi. How can I help you?" asked the short girl behind the window.

I ended up getting a small chocolate and vanilla twist dipped in hard chocolate. Dana ordered a scoop of superman ice cream. And my brothers both wanted a hot fudge brownie sundae topped with whipped cream and nuts. I'll never understand how they could eat those without going into diabetic shock.

Dana and I sat at one end of the table, staring at each other. I was glad my brothers came with me. They were acting as a buffer between the two of us. I don't think I was mentally ready for what Dana had revealed. She was now person number two to officially know.

"Hey, look." Callum pointed up at the tall lamp illuminating the patio. "The first fish fly of the year."

We all tilted our heads toward the light to get a glimpse. And there it was, its long and skinny body supported by its transparent paper-thin wings, circling the light.

"Not long before they're everywhere." Dana's eyes met mine. She wanted to say more, I could feel it.

"Yeah. Not long until we have to sweep their exoskeletons off the windowsills. And watch what we eat outside at night." I looked up at the light again, remembering that time my mom's friend Laura ordered an ice cream cone here and got a mouthful of fish flies after not checking before she took a lick.

Never had I been so glad that my brothers were nearby. They were my shield. And with them I could avoid the inevitable questioning that Dana had likely prepared for that night. *Maybe I should spend some more time with them. They are my brothers after all.* Maybe that's why they liked messing with me so much; I was their big brother. I had my dad when I was their age. Who did they have? Me. It was funny though, they didn't look much like me. We all had the same bone structure. It was our coloring that separated us. The twins took after our mom with their fair freckly skin, light hair, and pale blue eyes. Riley and I took after our dad's tanned olive skin, dark brown curls, and dark green eyes. Most people didn't believe I was my mother's son.

"Étienne, can we get Frankie a doggie sundae?" Callum asked, giving me the side eye after noticing the awkward tension between Dana and me.

"Yeah please," Niall added.

If I say no, she'll know I'm trying to avoid her.

"Sure." I sighed, then handed them some change. What choice did I have?

The boys ran up to the end of the line. "Stay away from the curb," I yelled, trying to avoid Dana's gaze.

"So. Tell me. What were you helping that guy Thad with?" She pursed her lips.

"It was nothing, Dana. Honestly. He came up to me in the parking lot after school and started talking. I didn't really know what was happening."

"But what was it?" She raised her voice.

"Dana. It's nothing!" I looked around, making sure no one else could hear us.

"So then why were you hanging out with him?"

"No reason. He just asked." I looked down at the ground through the small holes in the metal picnic table.

"He picked you up from your house, Étienne. Like, what the fuck." She clenched her hands.

"My god, Dana. Chill. He was nice. And looking for a friend. I guess." I wasn't sure how to explain exactly what happened. I wasn't entirely sure myself. But I know I shouldn't have told Dana to chill.

"Don't tell me to chill, Étienne. Just looking for a friend? Why would he want to be friends with you? What does he want?" Her eyes widened; she was starting to get angry but wouldn't tell me why.

Dana's words stung. *Why would he want to be friends with you?* To myself I thought, *Why wouldn't he want to be friends with me? Why are you friends with me, Dana?* "Oh, so I'm not allowed to make new friends? What was your advice, Dana? 'Talk to people.' Isn't that what you said? Aren't you making new friends without me too?" I clapped back.

Where was her anger coming from? And why did she dislike him so much? From what I gathered, he probably treated her the way he treated me over the years; we were invisible to him and his friends. Yeah, that was shitty. But no harm was done.

"Okay. Yeah. Talk to people, Étienne. But watch out for him," she warned, finger pointed inches from my face.

"But what has he done to *you*? Why are you warning me, Dana? Please." I needed to know why she demanded I watch myself around him.

"Look! They even put a doggy biscuit on top," Callum exclaimed as they neared us.

"Can we go now? Before Frankie's ice cream melts?" asked Niall.

I turned to Dana, the look of anger still hanging over her face. I gave her a small mournful grin. Were we nearing the end of our friendship? Were we growing apart? I was feeling uncomfortable being around her since her comments on our way to Cedar Point. But I'd hoped we would still be friends.

"See ya later, Dana." My brothers waved as we began heading back.

I turned to give her a wave but a vibration in my pocket stopped me. It was Thad. *Hey, are you working tomorrow?*

No. Want to do something? I replied.

TUESDAY 10 JUNE 2008

10

CLUMSY

I woke up later than usual the next morning. I'd spent a few hours the night before putting together a new playlist on my laptop to sync to my iPod. I had always listened to albums in full, but finally decided to take my favorite songs from each album I owned and put them together. Yes, I know people have been doing that since forever. You don't have to laugh at me. I stayed away from it because I always thought of it as an insult to the artist. They created and arranged their album the way they wanted it. Who was I to change that?

Thad and I texted each other through the night. He had practice with his hockey club late the next morning and told me one of the building attendants owed him a favor. Why? My imagination ran wild. He told me the attendant was going to let him use the ice rink for an hour right after practice.

That's cool. What are you going to do there? I texted, pretending I didn't already know he was going to ask me to come skate with him, which he ended up doing. The problem was, I'd never skated on ice in my life. And I didn't own any ice skates.

It's okay. You look about the size I was two years ago. You can use my old skates, he wrote.

What do you mean I'm the size you were two years ago? Have you been staring at my feet this entire time?

His message made it seem like I was much smaller than he was. That was not the case. He was about an inch taller than me, and yes, he was a little more muscular than me—most guys were—but there wasn't that much of a difference in our sizes.

I knew he wasn't going to take no for an answer; he wanted me there. I was worried I'd look like an idiot slipping and falling all over the place. But I wasn't about to pass an invitation into his life. I definitely wanted to be there with him.

We both agreed that I'd meet him at the civic center after twelve thirty, giving him enough time to do whatever it is hockey players do right after practice. Shower, obviously. He wanted to pick me up, but I said it would be a waste of gas and that I could get a ride, which was a lie. I decided I would walk there. The civic center was about two miles from where I lived.

It was a nice day, like most Michigan summers. The sky was slight overcast, which I liked anyway as it makes the trees look greener. And I do enjoy walking.

"I'd hate to live here," I said to myself as I studied the houses situated directly on the main road. Wouldn't you? Imagine opening the front door and your dog running out onto the main street. Even the sound of cars passing by in the middle of the night would be irritating.

The sudden siren of a cop car approaching from behind me made me jump. I looked at my phone to check the time. Fortunately, I'm a fast walker so it didn't take me long to get there. And by the time I was able to see the parking lot, it was nearly twelve thirty and most of the cars were gone.

Good. Not really in the mood to see people I might know anyway.

"Hey." He waved before coming in for an awkward hug, the

smell of his shower gel forcing me to prolong the hug a few more seconds.

I looked up at him as he unraveled his arms from around me. His silvery blond hair was messy and still damp. *So, he does do his hair.*

He already had his skates laced, making him tower over me. There was something different about him this time. He was more relaxed. Like he finally let out a deep breath he'd been holding in. His body wasn't so stiff. He wore jogging shorts that ended midway down his thighs and a T-shirt that had its sleeves ripped off, exposing his upper arms and the sides of his chest. Normally I hated when guys wore sleeveless shirts, they look trashy to me. But I guess he pulled it off.

He led me to the bench bordering the outside barrier of the rink and handed me his old skates to put on, which were surprisingly a snug fit. He removed the guards from his blades before removing mine, then helped me up and onto the ice.

"I have to be honest. This is terrifying. I've never been on ice before. Well, at least not on purpose." I was holding on to his arms, shivering.

"Here, let me help you," he announced, pulling me in closer to him.

He put one hand on my upper back, the other on my chest. The same way my dad used to when I was a kid when he would scold me for slouching. "Straighten your back. Okay, look forward. And then bend your knees a little bit."

How does bending my knees a little help with balance? "I probably look like an idiot," I said.

But he was right. I was able to hold myself upright. He let go of me, telling me to put my arms out slightly for balance. Then he showed me how to move forward by first taking small steps. Alas, I failed on my first attempt. My feet flew out in front of me.

"I got ya." He jumped after me with his arms out before I landed on the hard ice.

"You all right? You didn't have to jump after me like that," I said, holding on to his arm for balance. He waved as if it was nothing.

"All good. Let's try something else then," he laughed.

I swear I was stronger than I seemed. I was a swimmer and a runner, after all. The slippery ice, though, *that* was completely foreign to me. Even in the frigid winters of Michigan I'd avoid walking on the ice-covered pavement for fear of falling back and breaking my ass. My sister once slipped on the ice and severely bruised her tail bone. She could barely walk for days, and even had a hard time sitting. I can't imagine how figure skaters and hockey players cope with falling the way they do.

After helping me back on my feet, Thad's hands latched firmly on my hips as he guided me forward, encouraging me to take little steps. I'd be lying if I said that this didn't turn me on. His guidance distracted me more than it helped, but I eventually got the hang of it and slowly inched my way across the ice without his support.

"Okay. It took me over a half hour to move a few feet." I started to feel embarrassed. "I swear, I'm not this uncoordinated. Take me to a pool and you'll drown trying to catch me," I added. This time I winked.

"You're fine. And I'm sure you could outswim me," he replied, trying to comfort my bruised ego.

He supervised me for a few more minutes so I wouldn't fall, then sped off, flying over the surface of the ice. He began to skate backward, circling me before he added a few small jumps, which made my head twitch, almost losing my balance.

"You know how to jump?" I asked.

"Uhh, a little. I take figure skating lessons. It helps with my hockey." He put his arms out, swooshing backward.

"Oh. Really?"

"Yeah. Figure skaters train for strength and flexibility on the ice, not just speed. Which really benefits hockey. At least that's what my coach tells me."

"That's interesting." I really was interested. He didn't look like the type of person who'd try figure skating. *Am I stereotyping again?* "You really like being on the ice, don't you?"

"I do." He smiled, showing his perfect teeth. He then charged forward and swiftly passed me, nearly knocking me over. When I say nearly, I mean that he was several feet from me. I almost fell over on my own accord in fear of him approaching me at such a speed.

"Hey, can I ask you something?" I whispered as he grabbed on to me again.

He helped me back to the bench where I could finally remove the skates from my fatigued feet. My legs began feeling like jelly and I didn't think I would last any longer on the ice.

"Do you know Dana? From our grade?" I asked.

He squinted. "Um. Yeah, I think I do. Why?"

"Nothing really. She's a friend of mine and she doesn't seem to like you much. I haven't told her anything about you. I remember her making a comment once when you passed us in the cafeteria." I lied about the second half, but I needed to know. And I didn't want to tell him the whole story. There had to be something between the two of them.

He looked confused. *Shit. I shouldn't have said anything.*

"Does she have an older brother?" Thad asked. "He just graduated, right?"

"Yes. She does. But he graduated last year." I straightened to meet his eyes.

"We got into a fight once last year," he said. "I think he went to the hospital because of his nose," he added. "Why?"

"Oh. Um. No reason. I didn't understand why she disliked you so much when neither of us knew you." I tried to assure him there was nothing more to my inquiry. But now I was intrigued.

Why had they fought? Thad didn't seem like the fighting type. I mean yes he was in hockey, but he carried himself the way anyone who wanted to be left alone carried themselves.

"I really enjoyed this," I declared before he had the chance to ask why I mentioned Dana.

"Cool. Maybe we can do it again. Except, without you falling." He tried holding in a laugh.

I put on my shoes and tried to return his old pair of skates, but he shook his head and waved. "Hold on to them for next time. I don't need them."

Wow. Maybe he does like me, I thought as I watched him enter the locker rooms.

I went outside and waited on a bench near the entrance as he changed and gathered his things. It was a perfect day out—hot but not scalding. And the light overcast still blocked the intensity of the sun, though it was dissipating. I wasn't sure what he had planned for the day. After my embarrassing attempt in the rink, I wanted to ask him if he'd join me for a swim to redeem myself.

What's taking him so long? I leaned over to peek through the glass doors. There had been no sign of him for nearly twenty minutes. After a few more minutes, I checked again and saw four figures approaching in the distance. Two girls and a guy were walking toward the doors with Thad. I definitely recognized one of them, who was in the same grade as us and was probably one of his closest friends. Heather, the girl with the obnoxious laugh.

As they neared the door, Thad had this hard look of worry on his face. I fixed myself to an upright position, then took a deep breath. I was nervous. I had never spoken to any of these people before, and he was probably going to introduce them to me. I hoped.

Thad held the door open for his friends, staring at the few cars in the parking lot. He looked conflicted that his friends were there. *I get it. At this point, I think I'd be awkward as well.* Two of his friends moved forward as if they hadn't noticed I was there. Except for Heather, who side-eyed me. She looked me up and down, then stared forward as if she had something far more important to do. Thad followed them into the parking lot.

I thought he would turn back to me once they were out of sight—I *wanted* him to turn back. I wanted to see his face. He could have even sent me a text explaining that he couldn't speak. But he didn't. He continued to his car, started the ignition, and followed them out of the lot.

My jaw dropped and my stomach sank. How could he do this? How could he leave me there like that? *Dana was right. You are an ass.*

Rage took over me. I couldn't get away from that place fast enough. Where was I going to go, though? I was going to hang out with Thad, then I wasn't. And If I went home, I'd have to hide so my family wouldn't ask where I was and question the skates. My heart was pounding. Thoughts flew through my head as a stampede of emotions bombarded me.

I reached the curb across the street from the civic center.

"Hey. Étienne. Where are you going?" I heard. He was in his car, window down, approaching me. He sounded so nonchalant, so oblivious to what he had done.

I ignored him.

"Étienne?" He called out. "You okay?"

No. I'm not okay.

I turned to him but tried not to make eye contact. I could feel myself losing control. My eyes started to swell, a frog in the bottom of my throat. Which I know he noticed.

"Wait. What? Étienne, hold on. What happened?" He jumped out of his car as I turned again to walk away. "Please. I'm sorry. Hold on, Étienne." He grabbed my arm firmly, stopping me.

"I just... I need to go." I gulped, blinking and trying to push down the soreness in my throat. The wall had cracked, and everything was about to fall out.

"Please, Étienne. I... I didn't know what to do. I panicked," he stuttered, eyes reddening in unison with mine.

I dropped the old pair of skates hanging from my right shoulder. My body felt like it was breaking down, and I couldn't hold on to them any longer. I didn't want to hold on. "I know. I get it. I didn't think you'd drive away and not say anything. I just... I need to be alone for a little while."

Do you think I was being too dramatic? Maybe I was. I was used to people forgetting about me, but this was different. This time, it hurt to the core.

"Éti— Huuh," he inhaled loudly after picking up his skates. "I'm sorry." He exhaled as I walked away.

11

———

THE POOL

Was it possible to be so intensely angry with someone, yet still want to be near them? Was I blowing things out of proportion? I felt so conflicted. I wanted to forgive him and send him a text. On the other hand, I wanted to stay mad at him. *Snap out of it, Étienne. He probably doesn't even feel the same.* I tried to convince myself that he didn't like me the way I liked him, and that I had no reason to be so upset with someone I barely knew.

Instead of walking home, I went to the elementary school playground a few blocks away to blow off some steam on the swings. The clouds started to dissipate, exposing the sun's blinding rays as I swung my legs back and forth to catch some speed. I synced with the motion of my legs, pulling myself higher and higher until I got to a point where the chains began to buckle. *I probably should stop.* But instead, I kept aiming higher until my body had depleted itself of adrenaline.

Exhausted and panting as if I were Frankie after a long walk, I stopped to rest as the swing slowly began to re-center itself. I noticed in my peripheral a small car passing by the parking lot and slammed my feet into the mulch.

107

Is that him? Is he following me? I wondered, paranoid. I was the only person there.

Another car drove by. It wasn't him.

I was at the playground for about an hour. I swung as high as I could on the swings, then hung upside down on the monkey bars for a little while. Nothing like a head rush. Hanging upside down with my eyes closed helped me clear my mind, until all the contents of my pockets fell out onto the ground.

"Really? Ugh," I yelled, straightening my legs and landing upright on the ground.

Dirt had gotten into the creases of the earbuds attached to my iPod. I brushed everything off then repositioned my belongings into my pockets before throwing my headphones in to listen to music. *I wish men could carry bags*, I thought, commiserating about societal expectations.

What's funny is that as an adult, I won't be caught dead with my pockets stuffed to the brim. I'm always carrying a messenger bag or a small cross-body bag to throw my stuff in. I guess it's more acceptable now than when I was in high school.

I still wasn't in the mood to go home. Besides, my mom hadn't tried to call or text, which meant I had no reason to rush. I rolled my shorts up a little, removed my polo, and lay out on a clean patch of grass far into the field where no one would see me. Normally I didn't like exposing my bare upper body unless in a pool, but in this case, nobody was in sight. What better time could there have been to let my skin soak in the warmth of our home star?

Let's pick something else. What do I want to listen to? I paused the newly created playlist I'd synced that morning. I was in the mood for something different but didn't know what. I wanted to listen to something that would lift my spirits, though I was already starting to feel better from the sun's rays. I picked the album *Intuition* by DJ Encore, a Danish DJ. Most of the music he composed featured the singer Engelina, whose angelic voice always brought me out of a funk.

I only got to the second song before being interrupted.

"Hey," I heard faintly through the music.

You did follow me.

"Umm. How did you know I was here?" I looked at him, then pulled out the headphones and grabbed my shirt out of embarrassment.

"I, uhh. I was driving around and saw someone swinging dangerously high. And then realized it was you," he said.

I raised my right eyebrow. "Driving around?"

He sat down on the grass next to me, and I began to panic— although I couldn't tell if I was freaking out over the fact that he was looking for me, or that I was still shirtless in front of him. It also didn't help that his presence aroused me, causing me to hunch over awkwardly, trying to hide.

You can't put your shirt on now, Étienne. That'd be too obvious.

I handed him a headphone since I no longer felt like talking. I wanted him there. I had forgiven him. Talking it out felt more like a task. And I think he understood.

Thad inserted one of the earpieces and lay flat on the ground while I was still awkwardly sitting up, waiting for my excitement to go away.

"Hey, could I use your shirt to cover my face? Didn't realize how sunny it got."

Thank god, I thought to myself. I wasn't a religious person, but someone was watching over me.

I handed him my polo, which he used to cover his face, then folded his arms up and tucked them on his chest under my shirt. This gave me the opportunity to adjust myself and lie back down without him seeing anything.

We settled next to each other, though a few inches apart,

letting the music take over as the sun warmed my skin. It's funny how something that feels so good could be so damaging.

We'd passed through three songs before I realized that my favorite song on the album was about to start—"High on Life" —which was exactly how I felt with him, someone I really began to like, and even started to care about. *This is weird though. Should I change the song?* I opened my eyes and looked over to see if he had any reaction. If I had chosen that song first, my feelings would have been obvious to him. Thankfully it was only one in a lineup of seventeen.

We listened to a few more songs and then I remembered something; he was the really pale one. I should have been more attentive to that. I opened my eyes and turned my head to see what he was doing. He could have been sleeping for all I knew since my shirt was still covering him. His left elbow was peeking out from under the shirt, so I lightly poked it.

He jumped. "Yeah." He looked at me from under the shirt.

"Sorry." I chuckled. "Let's get out of here. Don't want your legs to burn up." I pointed to his blushing shins.

"Yeah, cool. Wow. How's that possible?" He pointed to my stomach, brows furrowed.

"What?" I looked down thinking a bug was stuck to my abdomen like that time during a cross country meet when a bee latched itself onto my leg in the middle of the forest and I couldn't stop. But it wasn't that. My shorts had slid down a little, exposing my tan line.

"We haven't been out here for that long. How'd you get so dark?" he asked, eyes glued to my stomach as if I'd spray painted my skin.

"My dad was from Lebanon. We tan easily," I said. *He was and so am I. Well, partially.*

"Lucky you. Do you ever burn?"

"Not really. Only if I've been out without sunscreen for several hours. But even then, it only hurts my shoulders a little."

It was strange. Up until that moment with him, I'd never had a conversation with another guy while shirtless. Even in front of my dad and my brothers I'd throw on a shirt before resuming a conversation. It was fine during swim practices and at my meets, as it was kind of an obligation. But standing there with him didn't feel as frightening as it would have been with someone else. I didn't feel the urge to cross my arms and cover my chest the way I did at Dana's house walking through the kitchen to get to the jacuzzi. Even after swim meets when I'd get out of the pool, I'd pretend like I was cold and cross my arms to cover myself.

He returned my shirt. And as I carefully placed it over my head, so not to mess with my hair, I noticed a little wrinkle in it. Normally a wrinkle in my clothes would have thrown me off, but with him in front of me, I didn't care.

"Where to, then?" he asked.

"Swimming?" I suggested, tilting my head.

"I don't have a suit. I mean I do at home, but..." He stopped, but I understood where he was going.

His suit was at home, where he didn't want to take me yet. And the public pool in our town would have ended up becoming an unplanned school reunion, something I wouldn't have wanted to look forward to either. But I had an idea.

"It's okay. I've got an extra suit. And we're not going to the city pool," I said.

"What other pool is there?"

"The school pool. I know how to get in without anyone knowing. And I never returned the lock I checked out, so my stuff should still be in the locker."

He grinned while raising his right brow. "How?"

"I'll show you." I waved toward his car.

I made Thad park behind the school outside the pool area. Inside, there was what most people thought was a janitor's closet in the short hallway that connected the men's locker room and the pool. It was actually an emergency exit that led to the roof of the pool and was almost never locked. We used the fencing that bordered the dumpsters to climb up onto the roof, then I led him to the door. It was still unlocked.

"How do you know all this?" he asked, eyes wide.

"Our coach was always late for Saturday morning practices. It gave us the chance to explore the school while it was empty. You wouldn't believe all the secret passages. There's even an underground tunnel that goes to the middle school a block away."

"That's not real. People have been talking about that for years," he contested.

"You sure?" I winked. No, I hadn't seen it, but with all the secrets my teammates and I had discovered, I didn't see why the tunnel would be made up. The middle school was only across the street, anyway. A short tunnel going under the street didn't seem that far-fetched. "Yes! They didn't cut it off." I clapped, seeing the lock on my locker still intact. Normally the school would cut off the locks that hadn't been checked into the main office by the end of the year.

My Speedo and my swim trunks were both still hanging along with my swim shammy and a towel. If you're wondering why I needed both a Speedo and swim trunks, it was because we trained with the trunks to build strength since they pulled us back, then raced with the Speedo to cut off a few seconds. Trust me, a few seconds was the only difference between first and last place during a swim meet.

"I, ah. I don't think..." He pointed to the Speedo in my hand.

"Don't worry. Here. This'll do." I dropped the Speedo and grabbed the trunks still hanging inside the locker.

I handed the trunks to Thad since there was no way my Speedo would fit him without exposing his entire being. Then I turned my back to him so I could change. I didn't care who he was, he was not going to see me completely unclothed. He did the same, but in the back of my mind I was hoping that he'd take a peek. I wondered if he was thinking the same.

We threw our stuff into the locker. I grabbed both of us a pair of goggles. Yes, I had plenty. Then I guided him through the maze of the locker room to the pool door. The locker room had separate exits for different parts of the school, and most people had never been through the pool exit unless they were on the swim team or forced to swim the mile in PE during freshman year.

"Oh. It's dark," he said, looking up at the high ceiling.

"Not that bad. I can go up and turn them on." I pointed up to the control room near the pool's main entrance. "But I don't want to grab attention if anyone is here."

"It's fine. I didn't expect it," he replied, following me to the shallow end.

I threw my shammy to the side before plunging into the water. The thing about high school pools is that they're cold. And it's on purpose. Training in warm bath water is not good for you, which is why swimmers always jump in as fast as possible to get over the initial frigid shock. Thad on the other hand was not ready for this and decided to slowly inch his way down the ladder.

"This is horrible," he wailed. I knew that feeling: The coldness of the water feels like knives stabbing your skin.

"It's better than burning your skin outside." I laughed.

He finally submerged his body, save his head, and let go of the ladder. But by the time he turned to face me, I was gone. I had fastened my goggles in the time it took him to descend the ladder and began swimming down the deep end of the pool, following the sloping tile to the dark depths of the diving well. I turned once I reached the bottom and saw him promptly climb out of the pool. And as I began to slowly float up, his figure appeared above me on the diving board, and he jumped before I broke the surface. He landed in a pencil dive inches from me, plunging into the depths. He reached up and grabbed my leg with his firm hand. He let out a thunderous laugh, emitting enough bubbles to momentarily erase his face from sight. But I needed some air.

I reached the surface before he did and took a deep breath, then looked up at the main entrance to make sure no one was there.

"Ope. Sorry," he spat, breaking the surface of the water mere inches from my face.

Sure you are.

"See. It's not that bad once you're in." I giggled.

"Are you kidding? It's still freezing."

"Then let's keep moving around." I submerged myself and started swimming toward the ladder.

After horsing around on the diving board, I showed him the few dives I knew. I really wanted to learn to dive but my coach wouldn't allow it since I was one of the few swimmers with endurance. She would force me to blow all my fuel on the few longer races before the divers competed.

I grabbed kickboards from the little shed next to the bleachers for both of us so we could relax and flutter across the surface to catch our breath.

"So, what's your family like?" he asked as I was trying to teach him to flutter and not awkwardly kick like a soccer player.

Didn't we already go over this? I submerged my head for a second before reemerging to answer. "Well, there's my twin little brothers who are kind of a pain. More so Callum though. Niall just follows along."

"I wish I had a brother," he said, continuing to make too much of a splash with his feet.

"You'd say differently about these two. But ah, then there's my younger sister Riley. She goes here. But you probably wouldn't know who she is." I shook my head.

"What's she like?" He looked me in the eye as we turned and kicked off the pool wall.

"She's fine, I guess. She's been getting into my business lately and telling my mom things she shouldn't, which is really annoying. And my mom always makes a big deal about me, so now I've been trying to stay away from them both."

"My sister used to do that when we were a lot younger. I don't think she cares anymore now that she's going off to college. We are kind of close, though."

"Yeah, see. We always got along. I think her boyfriend is kind of a negative influence. I don't really like him." I rolled my eyes.

"I wish I had younger siblings. It's just the two of us," he said.

He talked about how his parents constantly pressured him to push further in hockey. And how his older sister would defend him when his parents were being unreasonable. "Now she wants to go away to college next year. What am I going to do?"

"You could call me. If you wanted," I replied without thinking. *What is wrong with you, Étienne. How much creepier could you be?*

"I could." He laid his head on the kickboard, facing me.

We drifted across the water for a few more laps in silence, living in the moment and splashing each other. The sadness and rage I felt earlier in the day after the ice rink faded away as if it never happened.

"What about your dad?" He broke the peaceful humming produced by the circulation system hanging above the pool.

No. Not that. I was not ready for that. His eyes widened as I felt the color leave my face.

"Um. My uhh... My dad died last year."

"Oh. I'm sorry. I didn't—"

I waved and cut him off before he could finish. "It's okay. I don't talk about it much."

"Why not. You need to let it out sometime," he replied.

I need to let it out sometime? When did you become a therapist?

"Sorry. That was pushy," he said.

"No. It's all right. You have a point. I'm not sure how to talk about it. He made a choice in his life, which ended up killing him. He chose to do it, and it took him away from us."

"What happened?" He lifted his head off the kickboard.

"Well..." My voice cracked. "He was a heavy smoker and had been since he was a teenager."

"Oh." He tightened his facial muscles, moving his ears back a smidge.

"I hated it. Actually, we all hated it. And we all begged him over the years to quit. I even once infuriated him by destroying the freshly packed cartons of cigarettes my aunts and uncles sent him from overseas."

"Yeah. That probably didn't go down well." Thad's kicking started to become less noticeable.

"It didn't stop him. My dad had two choices when he got the news from the doctor: pick us or pick his bad habit." My throat cracked, becoming sore like it did earlier. "He had more than two choices if you think about it. There were four of us, actually five including my mom. He still chose the one over the five."

"It's okay," he encouraged as I hesitated to continue.

"The end was slow. And horrible. And painful. He could barely breathe and continued to sneak in a cigarette while hooked up to oxygen." My eyes started to hurt. *How stupid could you be to do that, though? Light a cigarette next to a canister of oxygen.* "He chose his little accessory over us until his last day, while my mom and I took care of him and cleaned up his sick." I felt myself cracking as my eyes swelled even more. And a strong feeling of grief and regret fell over me as I realized that I ended up hating him. I loved my dad, but his actions turned that love into worry, then into hate.

I hadn't noticed that I let go of the kickboard and was standing motionless in the middle of the pool. I'd never told someone how I felt about my father's death. Not even Dana.

The hatred and sorrow mixed with the realization of what I had said out loud, it was too much for me to handle all at once. My watery eyes began to weep, and I couldn't hold it in any longer. *Why am I doing this?* I thought to myself as I headed toward the edge of the pool. *Get yourself together, you idiot.* I needed to get out of there. This was far too much to handle, especially out in public.

But I never made it to the edge of the pool. Thad reached out for me and pulled me in. He wrapped his arms around my back and his warm body held tightly to mine. I was wrapped in a much-needed blanket, a comforting sensation I didn't know I wanted so badly.

This only lasted for a short moment before I came to, understanding that I was in the grip of this beautiful person who had approached me only a week earlier. I pulled my head up and he loosened his grip, letting me step back.

"I, ah. I'm sorry. That was really embarrassing," I said. *What was I thinking? I need to get out of here before I expose myself even more.*

"No. It wasn't," he replied.

12

WHO'S P. ANTOINE?

Taking Riley and the boys to Grandma's for dinner. Where are you? Wanna come? my mom texted as Thad and I were changing in the locker room.

Went swimming. Go ahead, I'll find something at home, I wrote.

I stood in front of my locker as Thad tied his shoes after I pulled out all of my belongings to take home. I didn't want to chance the school doing a summer sweep and throwing my stuff away. He sat on the bench for a moment as I folded my suits and towels, then I tucked my goggles and ear plugs into one of the towels since my swim bag was sitting at home, under my bed. I threw everything together under my arm, then noticed that he was looking at me. He was still seated with his elbows resting on his knees.

"It's okay you know. You don't have to worry about it," he said, noticing that I had been eerily mute since leaving the pool.

"I, uhm. I didn't expect that to happen. I'm sorry for putting you in that position," I stuttered.

I really was sorry. How awkward must it have been for him

to see me lose my shit, then have to console me. In the cold pool. Skin to skin.

"So, uh. Do you still want to hang out? If that's not too embarrassing." He raised an eyebrow, a grin appearing on his mouth.

I don't think I'll ever meet a guy quite like this one.

"No one's going to be home for a while. We can head to my place. I've got food." I wasn't sure how he'd take an invitation to my house, especially after what had happened in the pool only moments before.

"Will the famous Frankie be there?" he asked.

I nodded.

Thad parked two houses down from mine, which confused me since the street was mostly empty. *Maybe he's being cautious. I'd do the same.* We entered through the side door and into the family room where my mom kept Frankie gated. We almost always put a gate up in the entrance to the rear living room before leaving so Frankie couldn't get into things. We once thought he was dying because he had jumped on a kitchen chair, then onto the counter and ate an entire chocolate cake. I'll never understand how his little body pulled through that.

I opened the gate to let Frankie out but was ambushed by Thad trying to get into the room. He threw himself onto the floor as he saw Frankie step out of his bed to stretch, his tail wagging profusely. My dog wiggled his long body toward Thad's face.

"Who's a good boy? Yes, you are," Thad repeated after finding the squeaker he bought in Frankie's bed.

Dogs will always bring out the kid in you.

"My parents won't let us have a dog," he said, pulling my dachshund onto his chest.

"I'll go get us something to eat."

He decided to remain on the floor with Frankie, so I went to the kitchen to find anything in the fridge to eat. My mom was one of those kinds of mothers who'd cringe at the thought of an empty fridge. She reminded me of my dad's mom, who'd offer to make us sandwiches with every breath she took. I missed her. It had been a few years since we'd traveled abroad to visit my dad's side. Sadly, only his eldest sister could fly over for the funeral.

Despite the fridge being full, there wasn't anything prepared. I pulled out a serving plate, on which I placed rows of sliced tomatoes, sliced cucumber, some olives, sliced Arabic cheese, and a dollop of hummus my mom and I made. Then I pulled out pita so we could make sandwiches with what we wanted from the plate.

"I'm sorry there isn't any meat. I'm vegetarian and my mom hides the meat. Her way of being considerate." I laughed.

"It doesn't matter to me. Vegetarian, eh?"

"Yeah. I watched this documentary and... Well, I'm not going to get into it." I waved my hand after realizing that the details of the documentary might scare him as it did me. I still don't eat meat even now as an adult.

"You didn't need to go through the trouble."

"It's nothing." I waved him off.

If there was one thing my father's sisters taught me during my time spent abroad as a child, it's that it was morally irresponsible to not try your hardest at being a perfect host while people were over. They even had immaculate sitting rooms in their houses, which you were forbidden from entering unless entertaining guests. I couldn't count how many times I was yelled at for wandering around in the dark, trying to admire the impeccable handmade furniture in their *salons*, as they called them.

"This hummus is delicious. Where's it from?" he asked.

"My mom and I made it."

"You *what*?" he asked, licking the side of his mouth. "Where'd you learn how to do that?"

"I spent a lot of time with my dad's family when I was a kid," I said.

"Wow. So, you travel a lot." He lifted his head and placed what was left of the sandwich on the plate.

"We used to. When I was a kid, we went abroad every Christmas and during summer break. But we don't travel much anymore."

"Do you miss it?"

"I do. But then when I'm there too long I want to come back. I don't feel like I belong there. Nor here actually. I feel like I should live somewhere in between. If that makes sense."

"Yeah. I think it does." He grinned.

He and I stuffed everything we possibly could from the plate into our pitas, leaving no trace of food. We had been skating in the early afternoon, then swimming afterward without stopping anywhere to eat. And trust me, swimming drains your body.

He asked where the restroom was as I began cleaning up the mess. I made sure to leave behind no trace of a second person being there with me.

Where is he? I turned around after loading the dishwasher and seeing that he hadn't returned from the bathroom. I peeked around the corner into the front sitting room and the bathroom door was open at the end of the hall. *Shit, he's in my room.*

"Thad," I said, dashing over to the end of the hall.

He was sitting on my bed reading one of my notebooks. "Your room is so clean. It's kind of scary."

"Please. Don't." I reached out to grab it.

"Who's P. Antoine?" He looked up at me after I yanked the notebook out of his firm grip. "Oh come on. Sit. Relax," he said.

Relax? This is my room.

The notebook was a science fiction story I created while daydreaming. I didn't know if I'd ever become an author. Or ever be able to write an entire book. But I liked creating stories. You couldn't imagine how often I'd zone out in class while creating a new story in my head. It was my way of escaping the world. I hadn't written much in the months after my dad died. I continued to daydream but chose to let the thoughts pass through me without writing them down.

"Well, uhh. P. Antoine would be the pen name I'd pick if I ever became a writer," I whispered.

"But you are a writer. That notebook is filled with writing."

"I mean... These are stories I made up."

"Yeah, and writers turn their stories into books and other things. Tell me about the story I was looking at. It said *Anori* at the top of the page."

"I don't know. You'll probably think it's really geeky." I was not okay with this attention.

"Try me."

I introduced him to a story I'd created while zoned out at work one day doing inventory for Jason. "This is going to sound so weird." I paused. "It's a story about a technologically advanced alien civilization that colonized a planet which was beginning to show signs of intelligent humanoid life."

The actual story I wrote takes place far into the future after the colonization. It recounts how these invaders disrupted the evolution of the original ecosystem. I'm not going to continue describing the details of my story, you'll just have to read it yourself one day when I finish writing it.

"Okay." He pursed his lips and rested his elbow on my bed. He seemed to think it was interesting but questioned me again on why I wouldn't use my own name if I ever became an author.

"I'm not sure I like my name. I mean, it's okay. But it's not a name I would have chosen."

"But I like your name."

You like my name? Okay, now you're really crossing the border. Maybe you do like me in that way.

I tried convincing him that P. Antoine sounded better in the mind of a reader than my name. I don't think he agreed though.

We sat on my bed a while longer in silence as he looked around and studied my room. I wouldn't say that my room was a representation of who I was. The cleanliness of it did represent me, but the striped baby blue-and-white wallpaper that clashed with the light gray shag carpet would not be what I would have chosen.

I looked around my room and thought about how much I wanted to change it. *This room is ugly. Why didn't I at least try to paint this a long time ago?* I thought. The fact is, I didn't spend a lot of time in it until the end of the school year. Dana and I had hung out so often over the years at her place, and my being on the cross country, track, and swim teams...and then having to take care of my dad for the last several months of his life... All of that together contributed to never really getting to know my own room.

As I moved my eyes to the right, I noticed something that nearly made me jump. Thad was no longer studying my room. He was studying my face. I turned my head toward him and met his analytical gaze. He grinned in response to the smile that unintentionally appeared across my face. I looked further into his icy blue eyes. He had a tiny speck of brown in his left iris. Like a small eye-freckle.

I wasn't just looking into his eyes, I was staring into his very being. And at that moment, I knew there was much more to this than friendship. I began to fall for this person, and I think he felt the same for me. He couldn't deny it now.

He put his right hand on my knee, which immediately sent chills through my body. I wanted to kiss him. I wanted to lean forward and throw my arms around him, forcing his lips to collide with mine. But I waited. I wanted him to make the move. I didn't want to be the one to ruin this, especially if it wasn't what he wanted. So I waited.

He moved his hand up closer to my inner thigh, stimulating my insides. This was it. He was going to move in. It was finally going to happen.

"Étienne, we're home!" my mom yelled from the side door, causing Thad and I to jump up from the bed.

"Argh. Why? They're not supposed to be home until later," I whispered loud enough for him to hear as I gave him a disappointed look. "I'm sorry," I added, looking over to him after hearing the thumping of my little brothers approaching my room.

"Étienne, you'll never believe what happened at grandma's. Oh, *hiii.*" Callum stopped at my door, studying the stranger in his older brother's room.

Niall popped up behind him. "Hello. Who are you?"

"What happened?" I interrupted the twins.

"Mom and Riley got into a big fight about Nate. She's staying at Grandma's house tonight," replied Callum.

"She said 'I hate you' to Mom," Niall added.

"Well that's not very nice," Thad decided to chime in. "My name is Thad," he added, extending his hand to my little brothers.

"Are you my brother's new friend?" asked Niall.

"Yeah. The guy Riley was talking about Étienne going in the car with?" said Callum.

I looked over at him as a wave of anxiety crashed down over me. I couldn't imagine what he was thinking after my brothers mentioned that he'd been the topic of conversation. *This will probably turn him right off.*

"Alright guys, that's enough. He has to get home now." I rushed the two of them out of the room and grabbed Thad's hand, leading him through the front sitting room and out the front door.

"I'm sorry about that. And them." I sighed.

"They were fine. I wish I had little brothers to boss around. But I probably should get home." He grinned.

"Hey. I uhh…" I tilted my head toward my house, trying to bring up what we were about to do.

He understood. "It's cool. Not like today's the last time we'll see each other."

Please take me back to that moment, I thought, watching his lips as he spoke. "Yeah, you're right. Text me later?" I suggested. *Where is this boldness coming from?*

"Yeah. Um. Hold on a second." He ran up and grabbed my arm before I could turn back.

He explained that his seventeenth birthday would be on Thursday and his family was throwing a small party for him; he invited his school and hockey friends. "I wanted to tell you." He held on to my hand. "I don't want you to find out from Myspace and think that I didn't want you there. I want you there, but..."

I understood why he was telling me. At this point in our friendship, or relationship if you could call it that, I presumably would have done the same thing.

"You're only turning seventeen? I thought you were older than me." I shook my head in disbelief. "Well then I owe you a day after Thursday."

"I'll look forward to that." He winked, then let go of my arm.

So you DO like me.

"You look happy," my mom commented as I walked in the house. "Haven't seen you smile like that in a long time."

"Really, Ma? Stop." I raised my hand.

"So that was him, eh?" she inquired, sounding like our Ontarian neighbors. Then again, I guess southeastern Michiganders use *eh* the same way Canadians do.

"Mom. Stop."

I knew she meant well; she had made several unwelcomed comments over the years hinting that she knew I was gay, and that it didn't bother her. I wasn't up for it. If I confirmed what she was guessing, she would have made a big deal out of it. And I wasn't mentally prepared for that kind of attention.

"Sorry. I don't want to talk about it," I admitted. "But yes. That's him."

My mom was so moved by that last admission, you would have thought the words leaving my mouth had physically appeared from thin air and transformed into a smile that plastered itself to her face.

I rolled my eyes as I walked away. *You're a weirdo, Ma.*

WEDNESDAY 11 JUNE 2008

13

———

MA, COME ON

Hey. You awake? my sister texted before calling me at seven in the morning.

"Hello." My voice was raspy. "Riley. Do you know how early it is? Ugh."

"Yeah. Whatever. Can you go to my room? Please, Étienne," she begged.

Per her request, I went into her room and filled a bag with the clothes she directed me to pack, then went into the bathroom to grab her makeup bag. You wouldn't believe how heavy a teenage girl's makeup is. I'll never understand why she started using so much makeup. She didn't need it.

"Okay. Now get ready quick and bring it here before Mom goes to work."

"Riley. Are you kidding? Mom has to drive me to work before she starts. There's not enough time," I complained.

"Hurry up then. Come on, Étienne."

I threw myself together as quickly as I possibly could. Thankfully I'd already washed and styled my hair the night before. I didn't want to go to bed that night reeking of chlorine from the pool. Funny, isn't it? If you've got thick stubborn hair like mine, the best thing to do is wash and style it the night before. It makes it so much easier to manage the next morning.

"What? Étienne, where are you going?" my mom roared as I ran into her room to grab the car keys.

"Just dropping off some clothes to Riley. Be right back."

"Oh. Hurry up. It's the boys' last day of school and I still have to drop you off at work," she said as I exited her room.

It's time for a car of my own.

"So, what happened between you and Mom?" I asked my sister as she opened the passenger door. She was waiting outside my grandma's house and ran up to the car before I could even switch gears.

"Nothing, Étienne. Go. You have to go to work."

"You rushed me and now I'm early. What happened?"

She shook her head. "You won't talk about why you're being weird lately either, so leave. I'm not in the mood."

"You're welcome," I yelled out the window as she ran up the driveway.

I returned home to find my mom and my brothers waiting outside at the end of the driveway. I parked the car then moved to the passenger side so my mom could take command.

"You fed Frankie and let him out, right?" I asked.

My mom nodded.

"You made sure he was still inside and locked the door, right?" I asked.

"Étienne. It's my house. Why would I forget to do that?"

I nodded in agreement.

I'm obsessive when it comes to the well-being of my dog, and the security of the house. Especially after the one time I was home alone with Dana and a couple of kids from my street when we were eleven. We had been playing with water balloons in the backyard while the front and side doors were open. I went to the side of the house to fill more balloons from the hose when I thought I saw a figure move across the glass block basement window. It freaked me out so much that I ran to the house next door and asked old man Swanson to check it out. No one was there, but the experience rendered me paranoid for life.

Instead of dropping my brothers off in front of the school, my mom decided to park the car and walk the twins up to the entrance. Along with several other parents. I joined and tried helping my mom in taking some photos of them with their friends.

"Give me the camera. You don't know what you're doing," I whispered, pulling the camera from her hands.

"Hey. Let me do it. You're not getting close enough."

"Ma. I'm zooming in. You don't have to crouch to get a good shot. And do you remember how embarrassing it was for me when you tried using the camera at school?" I reminded her.

"Étienne. That was years ago. And it wasn't that big of a deal."

I side-eyed her. She bit her lip.

Yes, it was a big deal. My mom ran out of film at an assembly. This was before digital cameras were affordable. She asked another parent to take photos of me. How humiliating, right? The worst part was the next week in school when a kid in my class, who I'd never spoken to before, came up to me before lunch and handed me the photos. This made everything worse after knowing whose parent my mom engaged with.

"Come on. We're both going to be late." I lightly elbowed her.

"Just a minute, Ton— Étienne."

The photos took longer than expected and I had to nudge my mom again, guiding her step by step to the car so I wouldn't clock in late. I was only part-time. But still, punctuality mattered to me.

"I could've taken a few more pictures," my mom said as we entered the car.

"I took some good ones that I know will be in focus. It's

fine." I looked out my window, trying to remember what it was like going to that same school when I was my brothers' age.

"So. Is he coming by again sometime soon?" She turned down the radio while we were sitting at the stoplight a block from the strip center where the jewelry store was located.

I closed my eyes, face still directed toward the passenger door window, trying to take in the heat of the morning sun. *Why, Mom? Can't I be left alone?* I took a deep breath and turned to gaze in her direction. She had both her hands on the wheel, loose blonde curls covering the right half of her freckled face.

"What?" She twitched her head in my direction.

I looked forward as the light turned green and increased the volume of the radio as she flicked her right turn signal on.

"Hold on." She grabbed my arm as I unbuckled.

"Ma, I only have like a minute to punch in."

"What is with you lately, Étienne? You're always absent. You can't stand your brothers. You and Riley are at it. You don't talk to me anymore," she said before switching off the ignition.

I exhaled loudly, shaking my head as I looked up at the small mark on the car ceiling, probably from Callum's shoe.

"Is it him? You know he's welcome in our house."

"Ma, stop. I'm fine. Got to go to work." I opened the door, cutting her off.

"Is it your dad?"

That was my cue to leave. "All right. Bye."

"I love you," she yelled as I closed the door.

As I waited at the front entrance to be buzzed in, I heard my mom start her car and couldn't stop this inner voice telling me to loosen up. No one was in sight, which meant everyone was still in the back room opening and sorting through the jewelry vault. I looked through the door window, waiting to escape this weird interaction with my mom. But she wouldn't leave. *I guess I am being rude.* I rolled my eyes and rested my head on the door, exhaling. Then turned around and gave my mom a half grin and mouthed, "Love you too."

Finally! The door buzzed.

"I haven't seen you in like forever. Spill it. What's going on?" demanded Rhonda, following me into the back room as I clocked in a few minutes late. The owner Jason hadn't arrived yet, thankfully.

"Rhonda, we both worked on Monday," I said.

"Duhh. I'm not stupid. Monday feels forever ago though. Come on, did you talk to him?"

"I did. We hung out actually," I said, grabbing the broom from the kitchen closet.

I recounted everything that had happened between Thad and me the day before. The ice rink. The pool. What almost happened in my room. Her eyes widened and her jaw lowered, nearly reaching the hollow spot on her clavicle.

"Damn. He does like you." She jumped, but a customer walked in before she could continue. "Erhh. We're not finished." She rushed out onto the floor as Jason entered the kitchen.

"Fancy hair." He waved his hands back and forth.

It was in fact a good hair day. But this wasn't a compliment, so I ignored him and started toward the connecting back room where the jewelers polished, among other things.

"Hold on." He tapped me on the shoulder then handed me a list of chores for the day before adding, "Think you can handle that?"

I nodded. "Yeah."

Jason had me run a few errands for him throughout my shift, leaving Rhonda and me little time to continue our conversation. He handed me the keys to his massive Expedition so I could move unused junk from the back room to his storage unit across town. It took longer than expected. The owner's son was tasked with hauling all the Christmas boxes earlier in the year while I was cleaning the store and, from what it looked like, decided to shove all the boxes into the unit, leaving it to me to reorganize everything.

"Where were you? It's almost the end of your shift," he asked in a condescending tone upon my return.

"Half the stuff was piled to the ceiling right in front of the door. It almost fell over."

I tried to explain that his unit looked like it was hit by a tornado. But he didn't care and commanded me to continue working on the rest of the chores before I left.

"Right. So. What's going to happen next?" Rhonda sneaked into the back room for a minute while Jason was talking to an important client.

"Well. His birthday is tomorrow but we're not hanging out. I was thinking of taking him out to eat somewhere on Friday maybe."

"Gawd you're so cute." She pinched my cheek before rushing back onto the floor.

My shift ended before Rhonda had the chance to ask me another question. I could have clocked out and stayed behind for a few minutes to talk to her, but I wanted to leave. The owner put me in a bad mood while commenting on my lack of upper body strength when I needed help lifting a heavy box. It wasn't my lack of strength; it was a damn heavy box filled with precious metals.

My mom hadn't texted me yet to tell me she was there, but I didn't care. I needed to leave the building. I walked out into the parking lot to wait for her, then turned after hearing a voice call my name.

"Oh. Hey Dana." I looked up at her hair. "What are you doing here?" She was parked in front of the neighboring store, a gun shop. We hadn't planned on seeing each other.

"Your mom was running behind at the twins' school and called me."

What am I? A kid? Why was I left out of the loop? I really need a car. "Cool. Thanks." I forced a smile. "I like the purple," I said before opening the passenger door. *Guess you're going for the whole rainbow this summer.*

I was thankful she put aside what she was doing to come pick me up. But still aggravated. My mom could have at least kept me updated. How hard was it to send a quick text?

Dana had something on her mind. I could see it. We were about halfway to my house when she asked how I was doing after stopping at a red light. I was looking out the window, observing the dog in the car next to us and didn't respond until her second attempt. A snowy white Borzoi lay on its side across the back seat of the other car. I'd never seen one in person and was surprised how long their bodies actually were, compared to what I had seen on Animal Planet.

"Did you see that dog?" I pointed out the window. But she had already passed the car after the light turned green. "I'm doing fine. Not looking forward to the twins being off school now," I said after she glanced at me.

She looked at her rearview mirror, then to the radio and clicked the button to turn it on. *Oh. Well. She's bothered.* Trying to cut through the awkwardness, I continued talking, explaining that I was busy with work and maybe wanted to do something different with my bedroom. But the music continued to play.

She wasn't buying it. She knew me better than that. I could see her from the corner of my left eye. She had been examining me, probably wondering what I had been doing since we last spoke. Before this thing with Thad, and before my dad's death late the year before, Dana and I had shared almost everything. We were inseparable even when we got into fights. This was different.

I guess the wedge between us began as my dad was sent home from the hospital, when I started taking care of him. She let me have a little space that year after I started closing myself off. I don't think she anticipated the chasm between us to last as long as it did, though.

What was I to do? Should I have opened up to her about how much I liked Thad and risked her disapproval again? Or should I have remained silent until the strain on our friendship became more manageable? I loved my best friend, and I really liked this guy. So I decided I'd keep quiet about it and try to balance both of them. Things would eventually mellow, and we would return to normal.

"Are you still talking to *that guy*?" She pretended she didn't know his name.

I shrugged. "Kind of."

She scoffed as we pulled up to my house. "Whatever. Have fun with your new friend, Étienne."

"Are you still talking to James?" I asked in protest.

"Yeah. But that's different."

"How so?" I shook my head. But she didn't respond. "Dana! Having more friends doesn't mean I can't be your friend too. This isn't pie." I rested my arm on the center console.

She exhaled and blinked slowly as I tried explaining that nothing would change what we were to each other. But she sat there, now silently staring forward at my house after we parked in the driveway.

"Please Dana. Are we not allowed to have other friends?"

She didn't answer.

"Why don't we hang out on Saturday? I'm going to be off work and don't have any plans all day."

"Okay." She nodded and threw a quick grin in my direction before I opened the door. "Hey. Hold on," I heard as I opened the gate. I turned to see Dana's car still parked in my driveway. She was biting her upper lip. She started to say something, then stopped. "Never mind. See you Saturday."

"Thanks for the ride." I waved as she pulled away. "Good. We can get past this," I said to myself as I opened the door.

Before dinner that night, my grandma brought my sister home. She didn't want Riley staying there after they'd gotten into an argument about her boyfriend. I guess my grandma sided with my mom, which made things awkward at the dinner table. The only people who spoke were my two brothers. They decided to give us a detailed description of everything they had done that day in school. They recounted the photoshoot with my mom and me at the beginning of the day and then went on to tell us that they didn't have to do any work in class except watch movies and hang out. They were even given both a longer recess and lunch. My grandma asked them to pause while she ran to the bathroom; she was more interested in their story than the rest of us were.

"After lunch, we got to meet the sixth-grade teacher we're gonna have next year," said Niall.

"Yeah. And she's really pretty," Callum added. That's how I knew I was definitely gay—I was too afraid to say girls were pretty at their age.

The middle school closed the same day mine did, so the sixth-grade teachers decided to use their time off to visit the elementary schools and meet the new students they'd be teaching the next year. My brothers explained the little graduation ceremony at the end of the day, which most parents attended. The reason why my mom was late.

"You could have told me there was a ceremony at the end of the day, Ma." I pointed my fork in her direction.

"I didn't think you'd want to come," she said, pulling her blonde locks away from her face.

"You could've at least told me so I could call someone."

"But I called Dana for you," she responded innocently.

Yeah okay, Ma. You probably called her to get some scoop. I put my fork and knife to the side, no longer wanting to eat.

Riley, awkwardly silent the entire time, was the first to leave the table, descending the steps behind the kitchen wall into the basement as I started to collect the empty plates.

"So. Why were you fighting with Mom? And now Grandma?" I cornered my sister in the laundry room after I loaded the dishwasher. I didn't understand why she was there, though. I was the one who did most of the laundry in the house.

She gave me a dirty look and pushed me out of the way, the corner of her phone striking my chest. It hurt more than I thought it would. Then again, she was stronger than she looked. She had three brothers to put up with.

"I'll tell you what's going on with me, if you tell me why you're in such a mood," I said before she reached the top of the steps, which made her stop and think.

"You first." She started back down the steps.

Riley turned on the dryer so no one could hear us, and we both perched ourselves on the folding table. I started from the beginning. How Thad approached me in the parking lot. I admitted that I was a bit apprehensive and cautious when we first hung out, but that he turned out to be a great guy. She thought it was cool that he took me to a house party and was surprised Mom hadn't found out about me getting drunk. I did, however, leave out the part in the pool, and when we almost kissed. That would've been too much information.

"So you like him, right?" She raised her eyebrow, leaning back against the dryer.

I shrugged and grinned at the same time, too nervous to vocally confirm her assumption of my sexuality.

"All right. You next." I was determined to reposition the attention onto her.

Riley began by making me promise that I'd never repeat what she was about to tell me.

"I'm not the one who opens their mouth, am I?" I joked.

"Do you not want me to tell you?" She widened her eyes, palms facing me as she shook her head.

"Sorry." I crossed my arms. We had offered each other peace, so that comment was unnecessary.

I promised that I wouldn't repeat. And she commenced. But since she made me promise her not to tell anyone, I don't think it would be right to share her intimate life with you. All I can say is that I was utterly surprised. My mom caught her in a lie a few months earlier—a lie that I didn't think she'd be clever enough to construct. I don't even think I would've had the gall to fabricate a lie like that. The lie was so she could get her way with not doing a class project before winter break, not thinking that the teacher would contact my mom considering everything happening with my family at the time.

What confused me, though, was why she got into a fight with my mom. This lie happened a while ago. What could have triggered them to fight months after the dust had settled? Mom caught her in the house alone with Nate on her bed, his hand up her shirt. Which was the last straw for my mom.

"Eww. Riley. You're only fifteen. And Nate with that dirty hair. Ugh. I haven't even done anything like that yet."

"Yeah, well you are a prude, Étienne. You can't answer the phone without a shirt on and you even close your bedroom door to change your socks," she said.

I wasn't that bad. But she had a point.

Before turning off the dryer and returning to my room, I stopped and asked her what Grandma had to do with all of this since she got in a fight with her after spending the night.

"She's a crazy old lady. She was bothering me."

Yeah okay, Riley. I'm sure it was all her.

My situation was more hopeful than I had previously thought. Yes, my life was complicated. I was dealing with my own demons. But at least I hadn't overcomplicated it the way Riley had.

"Where'd Grandma go?" I asked my mom, plunging myself

into the sofa across from her loveseat. I went to the rear living room instead of isolating myself in the bedroom.

"You just missed her." She gestured to the side door.

My mom was watching the movie *Ever After*, the one with Drew Barrymore. My mom and I used to love watching that movie together. We also really loved anything Drew was in. I lay across the sofa deep in thought under an Afghan blanket my grandma made long ago. My mom had fallen asleep. *You can never stay awake during a movie, can you?*

It was close to midnight when the movie finished so I threw a blanket on my mom and grabbed a glass of water before going to my room. I wasn't going to wake her. She usually woke herself and went to bed. Trust me, she wasn't pleasant when not woken of her own accord.

Once in my room, I checked my phone for the time. It was midnight.

Happy birthday, I texted Thad then ran to the bathroom to brush my teeth.

You're awake? My phone dinged, then immediately started ringing. I had barely gotten the toothpaste lid screwed back on and had to sprint across the hall to my room.

THURSDAY 12 JUNE 2008

14

BIRTHDAY

"Thank you," he said through the phone as I lifted it to my ear.

Thad and I spoke on the phone for over an hour when he called me after midnight. I didn't want anyone to hear me, so I sneaked outside and hid in my sister's hammock. This time I brought Frankie with me so he wouldn't bark at or scratch the back door. As I lay there on the phone with him staring up at the bright moon, I thought it was strange that I had become a phone call person. Really though, most people my age would rather text than have an actual phone conversation. It's bizarre how someone can change simply by the influence of a person they like.

"I was thinking. Maybe I could take you somewhere nice to eat," I said, rubbing Frankie's belly as he lay on my chest.

"You don't have to. Where could we even go?"

Where could two seventeen-year-olds go out for a nice dinner? I didn't know.

"Well, I'm not sure. But I want to. I can look for a place." *Preferably somewhere far from our little lakeside suburb.*

He apologized during our phone call for not having invited

me to the party. The tone of his voice sounded like he wasn't looking forward to it anyway. I promised him it was totally fine since we'd recently started hanging out and his parents hadn't met me yet. They'd probably never heard of me.

"But um." His voice cracked before continuing. "I don't think you'd be comfortable here. So..."

"You mean with your friends?" I pushed myself forward to give Frankie room after he moved to my feet. Where was Thad going with this?

"No. My parents. They're not religious, but they are kind of closed minded." He lowered his voice.

"Closed minded about making new friends?" I pretended I didn't know what he was trying to say, but I did.

"It's not a joke, Étienne," he clapped back.

I wasn't sure if that was his way of coming out to me, without actually saying the words. But I chose not to look into it much further. I knew he liked me the way I liked him. And if that was outside of his parents' comfort zone, I wasn't going to push to come to his house anytime soon.

He continued to talk about it though, and how his parents had trained him over the years to carry himself with virility. Which he admitted was exhausting. I had a newfound respect for him. He'd seemed like someone who had it all—his own car, friends, parents who encouraged him and supported his athletic interests, despite steering him away from anything considered to be unmasculine. My eyes were now open to the thought that maybe everyone had it bad. Maybe everyone was battling something in their lives that only they could handle.

"At the end of the day they're still your parents. They'll love you no matter what," I tried convincing him, but I don't think it worked.

"I'm not sure about that," he stuttered.

"I disagree," I said before reluctantly adding, "that's not how it was with my dad. And he was a devout Maronite."

"A what?"

I imagined him pulling the phone away as he scratched his head. "It's like the Arabic version of Catholicism." I rolled my eyes.

"Oh. So, what happened then when he found out?"

"Well, I never said anything to him about it. But I know he knew from the way he spoke to me." My heart began to throb, and I didn't know if I had it in me to continue revealing this information.

I'd never told anyone this, but I explained to him how my dad had treated me throughout my childhood. I knew he loved me very much. He was one of those old-school Middle Eastern dads whose firstborn son was his pride and joy. But I was also the target of his incessant homophobic comments. He once walked in on me and Riley watching an episode of *Will & Grace* when I was fourteen. Instead of asking us what we were watching, he unplugged the TV as he heard Jack's voice, and then screamed about how faggots were doomed to the fiery pits of Hell. Encouraging, right?

"We weren't even paying attention to the show, though," I admitted on the phone. "I was playing on my Nintendo DS." Yes, I had one of those. "And Riley was painting her toenails."

During his sickness he stopped making comments about my mannerisms. I was the one taking care of him while my mom was at work. I don't think it would have been in his favor to do that to his only caregiver, especially since I'd missed a lot of school during that time. My grades were the one thing that made him proud. Especially when I did well in science as he wanted me to become a doctor. Like all Arab fathers. Well, all immigrant fathers.

"At the end of the day," I said, then took a breath as my eyes started to swell. "He told me that he loved me. I'm not sure if he changed his mind on the subject. But he loved me."

I tried holding back the frog in my throat while sharing this information with Thad, but it was hard, and my voice started to crack.

Thanks for last night, he texted me in the morning.

I ended the conversation that night, remaining in the hammock a while longer, stunned that he felt comfortable enough to share his insecurities with me. I never thought someone like him could have insecurities. He made me feel like I mattered, like I was being included. And this drove me to care for him that much more.

My mom had already left by the time I woke up. I decided I'd do nothing but hang out with Frankie for the rest of my Thursday. I gave him a bath then brushed out the tiny knots behind his long ears. That's one of the only downfalls of having a long-haired dachshund—the constant knots behind their ears. Their stubbornness is also a pain, but I could spend a whole day telling you about that, and I don't think we have the time.

I made myself scrambled eggs for breakfast after chasing Frankie around the house to try to dry him. I shared a small portion of the eggs with Frankie before adding salt and chopped chives to my serving.

I was interrupted by my brothers before taking my last bite. *Damn. Forgot they were home.*

"Ooh, can we have some?" asked Callum as he took a seat at the table.

Niall came in and put on Nickelodeon before sitting next to Callum. "I want some eggs too."

"Might as well make some for everyone," I said after Riley walked in and grabbed the orange juice from the fridge, setting it on the kitchen table.

"Move over!" Niall waved as Riley sat at the head of the table, blocking his view of the small TV on the kitchen counter behind her.

"Ugh." She grabbed the base of her chair and shuffled to the side a few inches while giving Niall the death stare.

Come on, Riley. Is it that hard to stand up and move your chair?

"Can I mix chives in?" I turned around with the rubber spatula in hand.

"No," Callum responded on behalf of them all.

"You guys have no taste," I whispered, placing the plate of scrambled eggs in the middle of the table. *Maybe I'll listen to music and go for a walk*, I thought after hearing the jingle of Frankie's tags as he entered the sitting room. "Riley, can you watch the boys while I take Frankie for a walk?" I asked.

She refused and said she was walking to meet up with Nate.

"Oh. So now you can walk?" I joked. "All right guys. Go brush your teeth and get dressed. We're going to take Frankie for a long walk," I announced.

"Can we get ice cream on the way back?" Niall requested.

"If you want ice cream then make your beds and tidy your room before we go."

I know. I acted like a fussy parent sometimes. But imagine how little boys would look and smell if someone didn't tell them what to do from time to time.

Callum and Niall insisted on holding the leash during our walk, which was annoying since the walk had taken much longer than anticipated. I find it interesting the way animals behave differently when around different types of people. With the boys holding on to the leash and horsing around, Frankie too decided to wander back and forth smelling everything that emerged a few inches from the ground. But when I would take him out by myself, he walked in a straight line and only stopped when he needed to relieve himself. Like he would mimic my way of walking—forward and with a purpose.

It was almost lunchtime when we finally turned around. I mentioned that we should go straight home to eat lunch, then get ice cream later, but they weren't having it. They had their minds set on ice cream.

"Fine then. If you get hungry before dinner don't come crying to me. Make yourself a sandwich. Or eat a carrot," I said.

They didn't care. They both wanted their hot fudge brownie sundaes with whipped cream and nuts. We couldn't get Frankie a doggie sundae since I didn't have enough money on me, so I ordered a small vanilla for myself and let him eat the soggy end of the cone once I'd finished the top part. The soggy bottom was my favorite part of an ice cream cone, but I knew he'd enjoy it as much as I would have. Besides, he had been drooling on my leg for far too long.

The twins ran into two of their classmates on the patio of the ice cream shop, who were also twins. They decided to sit with them and their parents, leaving Frankie and me alone on the only bench pushed up to the line of shrubs that separated the patio from the parking lot. I didn't mind. It gave me a moment to think to myself and look at the clear blue sky. *Perfect day for a birthday party.*

Thad not inviting me to his party didn't bother me, but it was still lingering in the back of my mind. I knew the party would have only included the family members and closest friends that his parents invited, but I felt like we had gotten to know one another enough that I would have been considered part of that group. At least in my mind. We had been getting closer day by day. I only hoped I hadn't been pushing him past his limit. I didn't want to scare him off.

I texted him as my brothers and I were guided home by our waddling wiener dog. *Have fun at your party tonight.*

Wish you could come, the reply read.

So do I.

15

YOUR CLOTHES AREN'T THAT TIGHT!

I need to get out of here, Thad texted.

I was on the sofa with Callum. Niall was on the floor flipping through the channels trying to find something to watch. My mom and Riley sat on the back porch with my mom's friend Laura.

You need to get out of there? It's 9:30 at night. Where would you go? Is the party that boring? I laughed, then sent a smiley face.

No. It sucks. My dad is being an ass. And my friends brought some random people with them who are being dumbfucks in the backyard.

A bit inconsiderate, isn't it? I replied before jokingly adding, *I'll come pick you up if you want.*

Could you? I can sneak out of here without them noticing.

What? Why would he want to leave his own birthday party? What had his dad done to make him want to leave so badly?

I ran and asked my mom if I could borrow her car to hang out with some friends. Obviously, I was going to hang out with him, and not *friends*.

"Okay. Hey." She extended her arm. "Text me if you're going to be late, all right?"

"Alrighty."

I ran to my room and changed into something a little nicer. I didn't know what would happen, but I wanted to look nice if I was going to see him on his birthday. I texted him that I was on my way then grabbed the keys from the kitchen counter.

I got into the car and started backing out of the driveway before realizing that I'd never been there and didn't know where he lived. I stopped the car and pulled out my phone to ask him for his address. He must have read my mind. It appeared on my screen before I finished typing the question. *Wait. What?* I thought, looking at the message. He only lived four blocks from me. Only four blocks from me and we'd never run into each other in the neighborhood after all these years. How was that possible?

I put out the headlights once I reached his street, then parked two houses away. I jumped at a bang on my passenger window as I pulled out my phone to text him. He had been waiting for me outside in the dark. I unlocked the door and he jumped in, then leaned over and kissed my cheek.

What just happened? I looked around and almost fell forward onto the horn. He'd kissed me on the cheek. Was this right? Was I dreaming?

"Hey." He winked as he pulled the seatbelt across his chest, the smell of alcohol radiating from his breath.

Are you drunk? I looked at him but decided not to say anything yet and drove away. My lungs felt heavy as I tried suppressing the thought of him kissing my cheek. I didn't know whether to worry that it was only the alcohol that pushed him to lean in toward me, or to let the natural feeling of happiness flow through me.

I glanced at him a second time, surprised that I hadn't noticed his outfit. He was wearing a pair of fitted dark jeans and a polo that clung to the grooves of his perfectly shaped upper body. Well, it was perfect to me. He wasn't buff like a jock. He was slim, but a muscular slim.

"My dad's an ass." His smile turned into a frown.

"Wait. What—" I started to say, but tears began to flow down his cheeks.

I pulled over before reaching Jefferson Avenue. I was going to take us for a drive downtown, the long way down the waterfront. But this was too distracting. I unbuckled and moved closer to him with my arms out. I embraced him and maneuvered myself so he could rest his face on my shoulder.

"Let it out. Tell me what happened. You can tell me," I whispered as he put his arms around me.

I wasn't sure if the alcohol was escalating his emotions, but I was certain that he was hurting. He let go of me after a few minutes. I restarted the car and turned onto the avenue as he began to recount what had happened between him and his dad.

His dad had been unpleasant that morning after hockey practice when Thad was supposed to join some of his teammates for figure skating lessons. Then there was the argument he had with his dad over his outfit. "There's nothing wrong with these clothes. I'm not always going to wear the same shit," he said.

He had gone to the mall and purchased what he thought were nice new clothes to wear for the party. His dad didn't share the same opinion and joked about him wearing "girly skinny jeans" while he was trying to hang out with his friends at the party. "They all laughed along with my dad." He hiccuped.

"Okay, first of all," I said, grabbing his left shoulder, "that was one of the first things I noticed when you got in the car. I love this outfit."

He smiled, wiping his wet cheek with the back of his hand.

We drove down the avenue bordering the lake, the windows rolled down, blasting the only CD of mine that was in my mom's car. It was a burned CD that Rhonda had made. I'll never forget how excited I was when she gave it to me. "Time of Our Lives" by Paul Van Dyk was the first song, and it fit the moment perfectly. I was happy to see Thad was enjoying it too. His right arm stretched out the window like a plane wing, and his other hand grasped mine.

"What kind of music do you like? I feel like I'm the one forcing you to listen to my stuff," I asked him as the song ended. We spent some time getting to know each other and yet we'd only listened to my music. What if he didn't like it? Was I being inconsiderate to his interests?

"Honestly. Shit," he replied. "No, really. Just dumb stuff that's on the radio. I never appreciated this kind of music until you introduced it to me."

You're trying to give me a compliment. I glanced at him.

"So, where are you taking us?"

"I'm not sure. I was thinking of a place that my coworker mentioned a while ago." I winked.

"What do you mean? Like to drink?" he asked, and I nodded. "But how?"

"There's a bar in Hamtramck that my coworker likes to frequent. She says the bartenders who work on weeknights don't really care and barely check ID. Wanna try to see if we can get in?"

He sat up, turned to me and placed his left hand on my leg as he smiled. "Let's do it."

We neared the downtown area, so I continued down the avenue and turned onto I-75 to get to Hamtramck. Rhonda had mentioned this bar to me several times over the last year. She was the type of adult who wanted to bring someone like me under her wing and corrupt them. She'd asked me to come with her more than once, promising that I'd get in without being carded since the stubble on my face at the end of the day made me look like I was in my early twenties.

I didn't much care for that compliment. Well, it wasn't a compliment in my mind. I hated my facial hair. Still do. My father's genes overpowered my mother's side when it came to that, forcing me to start shaving at fourteen. Even at seventeen, I shaved nearly every morning. And by the time I went to bed, the light stubble felt like sandpaper. Thad didn't look like he had that problem. His face was as smooth as I could possibly wish mine to be.

Is Thad's face going to hurt our chances of getting in? I glanced over and analyzed his face. We'd have to see.

Rhonda told me this was a chill bar where all different types of people went to enjoy themselves and to have a drink. She also told me there was a large room in the back with a stage where small bands would play.

"So she says it's on this street across from a liquor store. It has red window frames." We slowed down trying to find it.

"There." He pointed to the right.

I turned left into the liquor store parking lot. Rhonda also said that if I ever wanted to go to this bar, I needed to park in the lot across the street since it was well lit. We sat in the car for a few minutes staring out at the bar, then glanced at each other.

"You think we'll get in?" he asked.

I noticed a group of younger people across the street walking down the sidewalk and pointed it out to him. "If we hurry, we can probably catch up and walk in with them. We'd probably get right in."

He laughed as we hurriedly exited the car and darted across the street trying to catch up to the group. As they entered the bar, I held the door open for everyone and tried my hardest to make it look like we were with them. And it worked. The door attendant must have recognized them and let the entire group through, including the two of us.

"This is so cool, Étienne," Thad whispered into my ear,

stealthily wiggling his pinky through the fingers of my right hand, sending shivers up my spine.

Directly across from the entrance was the bar. It stretched along a mirrored wall, making the bar area feel much larger than it was. Long light fixtures, which barely illuminated the room with an eerie red glow, dangled from the unusually high ceiling. People stood and conversed at a few high-top tables at the room's center.

Thad and I decided to wander around and study the layout. The back wall of the bar was bordered with small booths; to the right of that was a dark opening to a black hallway covered with thousands of stickers that had all been half scratched off. This opening led to the large room, where bands would perform.

"Wow," said Thad. It was only a Thursday night, yet the bar was filling up quickly.

A cover band performed the best hits of the '80s. It was hard to hear with the band in the background, so I led Thad to the dark hallway connecting the two rooms and told him I'd try to order drinks for us both. He nodded and said he'd have a beer. I didn't really know what I wanted, but when I slid through the sea of people and finally reached the bar, the only beer I could recognize was Miller High Life, a beer my dad used to drink. I ordered two.

"It worked," I mouthed to Thad, the music now almost too loud for us to hear each other. It had worked. The bartender didn't even give me a second glance. She took my money and handed me the two bottles.

Thad clinked his bottle against mine then took a sip and as I brought my bottle up to take a drink, he pulled me in and said, "This is the best birthday I've ever had."

There'll be more. I hope.

Thad downed his beer as we were dancing, then grabbed my half-empty bottle to finish it. I didn't mind since I was the one driving and didn't want to chance getting pulled over in the middle of the night.

Coming home soon. Won't be too late, I texted my mom after remembering that she had asked me to let her know if I would be late. It was the least I could do after the stress my sister and I had been putting her through.

The room began to fill with more people as the band started playing "Dancing with Myself" by Generation X. I felt myself being pushed further into the room and closer to the stage. I reached out behind me to try to grab Thad, but he wasn't there. *What?* I looked around trying to point out his face in the mass of people who had just entered. He was nowhere to be seen.

Are you alright? I texted him, but there was no response.

I wanted to stay and enjoy the song, but I was afraid something might have happened. He was drunk. And we were both well under the age restriction. My mind started running wild thinking of all the bad things that could happen.

I tried inching my way toward the hall that connected to the bar but found myself in a maze having to walk around and find openings between people. Eventually, I gave up trying to be polite and pushed through yelling, "Sorry. Excuse me. Watch out."

The bar area was nearly vacant since everyone rushed to see the band. I found him leaning back in the corner booth with one leg rested on the banquette, sipping on a new bottle of beer. He saw me, pulled the beer down from his mouth, and motioned to come sit with him. He was happy to see me, though his eyes were droopy. *I think you've probably had enough.*

"You all right? I think we should leave soon." I leaned in.

"Leave, why? Just got another bottle," he slurred.

"I'll go get you a water."

"Wait. I'm fine. Come hang out with me. I want you with me." He grabbed my arm as I started to stand.

I got up anyway and went to the bar and asked for some

water; he really needed it if we were going to survive the ride home. Sadly, I was forced to buy a bottle since they didn't provide glasses of water. *Three dollars?* I rolled my eyes after reluctantly handing her the cash. I looked up at all the bottles of liquor hanging in front of the mirrored wall while she went to the furthest cooler to grab the water. *How can you remember what is what? There's so much.* She handed me the bottle and as I turned from the bar, my throat tightened in reaction to the sound of a fist colliding with a table.

"I'm not a fucking fag," Thad's voice erupted from behind me.

My eyes focused on him as he jumped up from his seat, staring down a man who was turned away laughing a few feet from the booth. Even in this dim red lighting, I could see his face was crimson with rage. He looked like he was about to collide with the older man. "Thad!" I dropped the bottle and ran toward him.

Clang. My head hit the tile floor after I intercepted Thad's attempt to tackle the person who apparently insulted him. It wasn't that hard of a thud, enough to allow a headache to cloud my mind as I coughed. My vision blurred as I blinked to refocus my contact lenses.

"Hey! Get back over..." Thad yelled before I felt his hands under my back.

The guy ran into the crowd at the other end of the hall as Thad helped me off the floor. I don't think the man expected Thad to charge after him like that. And I don't think Thad expected me to try to stop him. When my vision cleared, I saw that the bartender had picked up the bottle I dropped and was heading over to us.

Oh no. We're in trouble.

"I think you'd better head out." She handed me the bottle.

Thad furrowed his brows, his eyes widening. We weren't the

ones who'd started any trouble, but I cut him off as he started to speak. "Yeah. Let's go." I grabbed his hand.

"Are you okay?" he asked me. We had been sitting in the car for a few minutes sipping on water to try to sober up. Well, he needed sobering up. I needed to refocus after banging my head.

"I'm good. What happened in there?" I wasn't good. My head was pounding, and I thought I might have bruised my right hip. But I didn't want to exacerbate the situation by telling him about it.

"I just... I flipped." He grabbed his head before adding, "The guy walked by and called me a fag. Out of nowhere."

"It happens. But they're just words. You could have gotten hurt in there. Or worse, arrested for fighting in the bar," I warned.

The fact is, we were both teenagers in a bar drinking alcohol. Adding a fight to that would have made matters worse for everyone involved.

"But I..." He was trying to find the words to express his thoughts. "I'm not a fag. I...I can't have people looking at me like that."

And there it was—the truth. It wasn't the word that bothered him, it was the idea that people would look at him in that way. He liked me. I knew he did. The evidence was there to support it. But he felt insulted. Insulted in admitting that there was truth to what that guy called him.

I didn't respond and restrained myself from asking him further questions as I drove us home. If he didn't like the thought of being with a guy, then he didn't like the thought of being with me. Everyone deals with it differently, and some people deny it for years before finally accepting it. Hell, even I couldn't say it yet out loud to my family and friends. But facing the fact that the person you're falling for might be ashamed of being with you is a hard hit in the chest.

Our exit on the freeway was nearing and I had been facing

forward the entire time, music on low, trying not to catch Thad's eye. If he saw mine, he'd know I was upset.

"Hey," he spoke softly, placing his hand in my lap.

I looked over at him and forced a grin as his blue eyes met with mine. I grabbed his hand, then my eyes started to swell.

I don't want to lose you, I thought, directing my wish through the windshield and to the moon above.

16

DANA

Friday was kind of a blah day for me. My head still throbbed from being slammed against the floor. And I had to work the closing shift at the jewelry store without Rhonda, which was a pain in the ass. Luckily whenever she was there, the owner wouldn't bother me as much. She was one of his best sales associates. He needed her, and she knew it. She'd hold that over his head and get in his face sometimes when he was bothering me. She was like a mom, or an older sister. Have you ever had someone like that? Someone to look out for you like Rhonda did me?

I was expecting her to be there and wanted to fill her in on everything that had happened Thursday night at the bar. And Friday morning at my house, which I'll eventually tell you all about.

Eww. Why did I request to be off today? You need to tell me everything, she wrote after I texted her that Thad and I went out the night before.

The two of us planned to hang out Saturday afternoon so I could "spill the tea," as she would say. Though the term is common now in American vernacular, it definitely wasn't at that time, unless you spent a lot of time around drag queens. Did she?

I was supposed to hang out with Dana on Saturday. When she picked me up from work on Wednesday, the last day of school for the twins when my mom neglected to inform me that she wouldn't be picking me up, we planned on hanging out. She felt hurt that I had made a new friend. I understood that, and I wanted to assure her that our close friendship remained the same. Well, I was obviously wrong.

I spent Friday morning before work thinking about what Dana and I could do together. We could have hung out on the Detroit riverfront. Gone swimming and lay out on one of the many beaches of Lake Saint Clair. Dana liked baseball, which bored me half to death. But we could have gotten tickets to a Tigers game if she wanted. We could have even stayed at my house. I was sure my mom wouldn't have cared if we had one drink since she would be home. I would have even watched some *SpongeBob*, her guilty pleasure and favorite childhood show. Well, our favorite childhood show.

I was going to text her later in the day during my break at work, but Jason thought it would be a cool idea to have me take everyone's order and use my break time to run to the nearest Coney Island and grab lunch for the whole team. Of course, Jason had to order the most complicated dish on the menu, and then asked for substitutions, messing up the entire order. I spent almost my entire break waiting for them to correct the mistake before going back to work. He even had the nerve to tell me he wouldn't have taken as long as I had.

You really want a punch in the face, don't you? I closed my eyes as he stood there comparing my work ethic to that of an unambitious spoiled kid. Which I was not, I don't think.

Texting Dana had slipped my mind and I continued with my shift as normal, doing Jason's dirty work in the back room. There was still a lot more organizing to do with molds that were thrown into boxes over the years. There were thousands of them, rubber molds used to cast wax before melting gold into a ring, or any other type of jewelry. I couldn't understand why he wouldn't throw them away after a few years when ring designs and trends changed. Besides, he employed two full-time jewelers: one who made the molds and the other who melted the gold into them and then set the stones before polishing them.

Other than dealing with Jason, working at a jewelry store was interesting. Aside from being blinded by the gaudy, shiny decorations that littered the sales floor, the actual mechanics of the industry worked like a well-oiled machine. The ones who made the jewelry by hand needed intense upper body strength and hands of steel to deal with the heat and manual labor. They really are artists.

It was nearly eight o'clock in the evening when I realized it was time to clock out. I'd gotten through a few more boxes, but there were still several to organize during my next shift. I swear, looking back at all the molds I had to go through, you'd think Jason made me do it to laugh at me. I guarantee that hundreds of them had only ever been used once and would never be used again. I neatly put everything away, save the boxes that still needed my attention which I set in the corner. Then I entered the kitchen where the time punch machine hung on the wall next to the two-way mirror that surveyed the sales floor.

Where are you? Kayla texted.

? I responded.

When are you getting here? I can't be the only one helping Dana.

Only one helping Dana with what? *Just getting off work. Help Dana with what?* I shook my head, rereading her message. Dana hadn't mentioned anything to me. We were supposed to hang out on Saturday, not Friday.

"What's up? Why are you being weird?" she said when I called her outside of work. My mom hadn't arrived yet.

"Kayla. What are you talking about? Dana and I planned to hang out tomorrow," I said.

"Étienne, what are *you* talking about? Didn't you get invited to the Myspace group? Dana made it like a week ago," she said.

"What group? I wasn't invited to anything online." I pulled the phone away from my ear, brows raised.

"Stop being weird. Of course you were. She's throwing a party tonight. Her parents are up north again. Even James is here to meet everyone. You know, her new boyfriend. Like, literally everybody we know was invited."

The air escaped my lungs as if the twins were sitting on my chest, leaving me speechless for a moment. Did I miss the invitation? I didn't remember getting any notifications the last time I logged into my account, which I checked at least once a day. The last notification I got was the weekend prior when Thad requested to be my friend.

Just before I responded to this news, I heard Dana's voice asking Kayla who was on the phone. Kayla responded that it was me, then the line was disconnected.

I wanted to think it was nothing. It could have been a dropped call, which was common in the 2000s. I called back, and there was no answer. I then called Dana. *This is weird. Maybe she missed my name on her friends' list.* But she didn't answer either. Was I not invited? Was I not supposed to find out that she was having a party? The strain in our friendship hadn't stretched far enough for her to blatantly shut me out like that. There had been parties in the past that I had been left out of, but this was different.

This time I was left out on purpose. If this had been any other time before my meeting Thad and before her knowing about him, she would have invited me to meet her new boyfriend, even if I wasn't considered the house party type of person.

Am I that much of a killjoy? I thought to myself in the car on the way home with my mom. I began to panic on the inside as a sea of doubtful thoughts washed over me. Did my friends actually like me? Or did they remain my friends out of habit? We'd known each other for so long, they probably only thought of me as an accessory. You know? Like when a person is getting dolled up for a night out, then takes one thing off and leaves it behind before leaving. Had I unknowingly become that one unnecessary item left behind?

"You okay?" my mom asked, seeing through my pensive expression as I stared out the passenger window.

"When was the first time you realized you might be losing a friend?" I asked, knowing the question was more revealing than I wanted. But what did I have to lose?

"What do you mean? Who?" She straightened her back and looked at me before returning her gaze to the road.

"Ma! Nobody. Never mind." I exhaled. I should have known better than to ask my mom that question. She was going to make a thing of it like she would with everything else.

Although I'd had an amazing time Thursday night, and a great morning on Friday before work. I felt more alone that night than ever before. My closest friends were all together at my best friend's house. Without me. And the one person who I finally felt I could talk to wasn't in town. Thad was with his family across the state to check out a university his sister had finally chosen to attend.

I ended Friday night stretched out on the pavement of the back porch, listening to the playlist on my iPod. Frankie was by my side, belly up, his front paws folded against his chest, hind legs stretched out. And that was all I needed. The world could fall apart around me. I could lose everything. As long as I had Frankie with me, everything would be okay.

I felt a nudge in my side. It was Laura, my mom's childhood friend. She poked me with her big, tattooed toe, which always hung out over the flip flops she wore year-round. I looked up at her and she winked, lightly biting on her cigarette.

"Hey boo. Come on, get up," she demanded, taking a large puff of the cigarette.

"Would you put that cancer stick out." I waved my arm and pretended to cough. I hated the smell of cigarettes and always hassled her about quitting. I would say to her, *"Do you want to turn out like my dad?"*

We sat on the porch facing the back fence that divided our yard and the football field of my school. Laura took turns sipping on her drink, then sipping on that damn cigarette before eventually putting them both down to ask why I was hanging out alone in the backyard. My mom obviously mentioned what I had asked her in the car after work. Laura was a kind and selfless woman who became friends with my mom when they were in high school. She never had kids, but always treated us as her own.

"So, are you talking about Dana?" She turned her head.

I closed my eyes and didn't respond.

"Étienne. I know you even better than your mom does," she said as I raised my brow. How did she guess who I was talking about? My mom didn't even know and probably thought my question was referencing this new guy.

"My mom told you, huh? Yeah. It's Dana." I made eye contact with her, then looked out past the fence at the dark figures jogging on the track behind my house.

"What happened? You guys are supposed to be thick as thieves." She tapped her cigarette on the edge of the armrest.

I exhaled, then summarized the last week and a half with Thad, leaving out the intimate details and my true feelings for him. I explained how Dana had warned me about him but was also acting kind of jealous, and being hypocritical, that I made a friend.

"It happens," she said before I finished, blowing out a cloud of smoke that latched to her ear-length hair. "Sometimes a friend feels like they're losing you. It sucks. Ya know?"

"But the thing is, she isn't losing me. I want to be friends with her. She doesn't like my new friend and doesn't even know him."

"It'll blow over." She waved her cigarette-holding hand.

"She's having a party right now. I guess everyone is there. She never said anything to me. She didn't even answer when I called." I looked at Laura's face, her lower jaw slightly to the side as she squinted.

"That bitch," she murmured.

"She's not a bitch, Laura. Stop."

"Well she's not a friend. True friends don't leave you out." She puffed what was left of the bud, grabbed her drink, then got up.

"Look, boo. Your mom and I have had our share of fights over the years. But the one thing we don't do—the one thing we've never done—is let jealousy and secrets tear us apart."

I should probably tell Dana how I really feel about Thad then, I thought as Laura entered the house. Maybe she'd understand once she knew why I liked him, and the tension between us would fade away. But I couldn't. I couldn't tell her what was really going on without outing Thad. And I knew he was not ready for that. Hell, I wasn't ready for it either. Should I have risked losing a friend to protect finally finding someone who was interested in me?

SATURDAY 14 JUNE 2008

17

———————

TRICKED

"Hey love." Rhonda waved as she got out of her car and headed toward me on the porch.

Being that I didn't see her at work, Rhonda called me Saturday morning to find out more about my night with Thad. But since everyone was home, I didn't feel comfortable talking about it for fear of prying ears. I said I'd tell her about it during our next shift. She wasn't having any of that, so we planned to get something to eat since my plans with Dana obviously fell through.

"Hey. I'm ready to go. Where are we going, by the way?" I awkwardly hugged her from the first step.

"Go pack a bag for the night."

"Um. I think I have to ask my mom. I told her we were going to get something to eat. I can't just pack a bag and leave." I bared my teeth, unsure why I'd need an overnight bag when we'd only planned on going to a restaurant.

"Go. Don't worry about her." She waved me out of the way and headed into the kitchen where my mom was unpacking groceries.

"Rhonda! Hi." My mom opened her arms.

169

Rhonda was the only reason my mom occasionally liked coming into the jewelry store before the end of my shift; they both loved to chit chat. If Rhonda were closer in age to her, they would have become the best of friends. Which I think might be the reason my mom never questioned why she would want to spend time with me, a teenage boy.

I ran to my room and grabbed my swim bag from under the bed. *What should I pack?* I had no idea what she had planned. I knew to pack clothes for sleeping and my toiletry bag, but what about real clothes? I stuffed my bag with enough to last me a few days, just in case. And when I say "just in case," I don't mean there was a possibility of me spending more than one night away from home. I packed enough clothes so I could better pick an outfit once I'd learned what she had planned. Though I knew I probably wouldn't use any of it.

I threw my bag down by the front door, then passed my mom and Rhonda in the kitchen to grab Frankie and take him out. I knew my mom would let him out again before going to bed, but I wanted to make sure he got some exercise. I opened the back door, called his name and he came running from his bed in the rear living room. I loved the way his collar jingled with his waddle.

I greeted my brothers and their two friends who lived down the street. The four of them were kicking around a soccer ball behind the garage.

"Étienne. Come be the goalie." Callum pointed to the far side behind the garage where two large twigs were stuck into the lawn to imitate goal posts.

"I'm going out. Sorry guys," I said, apologizing for not being able to play since I was leaving for the night. "But can you do me a favor and keep an eye on Frankie?" I knew my mom would. A little responsibility couldn't hurt them, though.

"Fine," said Niall. "Now get out of the way so we can play."

"Be careful you two." My mom waved from the door as we entered Rhonda's black Zephyr.

I never knew how Rhonda convinced my mom to let me stay out that night. My mom was the kind of parent who'd let any of our friends stay for a sleepover. We, on the other hand, were seldomly allowed to stay a night away from the house unless we were with a relative. My mom was somewhat picky about the way we ate and who fed us if we weren't home. She labored in the kitchen every day after work to make us dinner and looked down on parents who fed their kids junk or frozen food. Which is why we would eat later in the evening than most families.

"Okay. So. Where are we going that I need an overnight bag?" I asked as she pulled out of the driveway.

"Girls' night. Duhh." She laughed, exposing her unnaturally straight teeth, then turned up the stereo playing her Tiësto CD.

She finally got her way. The several times I brushed off an invitation to her girls' night had pushed her over the edge, so she tricked me. It's not that I never wanted to go. I did. The fear of being the youngest person there stopped me. Also, up until my drunken night with Thad at his cousin's party, I was afraid of my reaction to drinking alcohol. You know how some people become angry or mean after drinking, and other people become talkative and let out all sorts of secrets they would have never revealed if sober? Yeah, that's what scared me. Fortunately, my night with Thad helped me overcome that fear. I'd learned that I was a silly drunk who sat in the corner outside and fell asleep. That seemed pretty safe.

Rhonda turned down the music. "I want you to make that hummus you bring to work sometimes. The girls would love it." She winked.

"Sure. But you'll have to go to this market that's out of the way. And do you have a food processor?" I said. It isn't easy if you're going to make it yourself. Not only do you need the ingredients, but you also need the right tools.

Her brows scrunched, eyes looking up. "Yeah. I have one."

I twirled my pointer finger. "Okay. You'll have to turn around and head down toward 9 Mile Road then."

She dropped me off at the little Middle Eastern market located in the modest downtown area of our suburb. And as I closed the door, she opened the window and threw one of her credit cards at me and told me to get whatever would be good for the night. "Take it. You're not paying for anything."

"Do you want me to get other stuff? I can put out a spread of little finger-foods." I leaned forward and touched her arm hanging out the window.

Her eyes widened. "Are you kidding? Do it!" she replied, then drove off to buy liquor.

From what I had heard, some of her friends usually brought store-bought platters and frozen junk that were thrown in the oven or the microwave. Rhonda needed to up her game, and I'd be the one to help her with that.

"*Ahlan. Ahlan ya habibi.*" The little old lady who owned the market welcomed me into her arms and gave me three pecks, alternating cheek to cheek.

"*Hi amtou. Kif sahtik?*" I replied, asking how her health was. I'd been around the Arabic language all my life and understood it, but usually replied in English out of fear of making a mistake. *Amtou* means aunt. She was technically not my aunt, but she was related to my dad. In any case, with our culture you call your elders aunt or uncle out of respect, even for those who aren't related to you.

The family that owned this market were distant cousins of my dad, though I'm not sure how they put it together and how they coincidentally ended up in the same suburb on the other side of the world. This market was like a home away from home for him when I was younger. As a child, I spent hours in the back room with my distant cousins running through the aisles of herbs and spices while the adults sat to drink coffee and chain-smoke by the back door. The best part of hanging out there was the amount of expensive pine nuts I could eat without anyone knowing. I'd stick my arm in the massive storage bins and grab hands full. That sounds unsanitary now that I look back, but they were my favorite. There's something about the slight metallic aftertaste of pine nuts that I could never resist.

At the market, I grabbed enough ingredients to make my paternal grandma's Fattoush salad. Then grabbed a few cans of chickpeas and a container of tahini along with a few other items that would be used for the hummus. I won't tell you what they are for fear of my mother's wrath. My dad's mom taught her how to make it and made her swear that she would guard the recipe with her life. I also grabbed two bags of pita among some other things to make mini pita sandwiches for everyone to snack on.

"Étienne, this is a lot," Rhonda said as I was preparing food.

"Is it too much? I'm sorry. I'll pay you back."

"Nonsense. Here, let me help you," she replied, rolling her eyes.

I waved her off. "Continue what you were doing. I got this."

The problem is that she was the one who needed the help, not me. She was still tidying her condo and grabbing extra chairs from the basement to place in the living room. People were supposed to be arriving shortly and none of the alcohol was cold. Most of it was still sitting on the kitchen floor next to the large cooler she had me drag in from her garage. One of her friends volunteered to come early with bags of ice and to help set up, but that friend hadn't arrived yet.

Eventually, Rhonda's friends trickled in one by one, some bringing alcohol with them and others bringing food that was obviously prepared by the staff of the local Kroger or Village Market. It was perfectly fine, though. The food looked really appetizing. Yet some of her friends dropped their belongings on the kitchen counter or the dining room table and left it there. To

Rhonda's relief, I took charge of setting up the food. I unpackaged everything and arranged it on the dining room table, circling the pita sandwiches I had made and the bowl of hummus resting in the middle of a platter filled with toasted pita chips. Trust me, it isn't that hard to go the extra mile.

Rhonda's friends were quite fun. They were all nice to me and were excited to finally meet "little Étienne," telling me how much my name would come up when Rhonda was talking about work.

Little Étienne, eh? I'm 5'10 without shoes, that's not little.

"Don't you listen to Jason. He's an ass," one of them whose name I didn't catch yelled from across the room.

Initially, I didn't want to drink alcohol that night. For a seventeen-year-old to have been drinking twice within a two-week period—three times if you include Dana's jacuzzi—seemed to push it. But by the time I was introduced to each of Rhonda's friends who walked through the door, I had been offered so many drinks and shots that my mind felt like it was a buoy floating back and forth within my skull. These girls wouldn't take no for an answer. Should I be calling them women? They were older than me. Is that disrespectful to have been calling them girls?

But seriously though, I couldn't handle drinking as much as they were. Then again, they were older than me.

After filling a plate with some food and grabbing a can of Vernors, I headed to a chair in the corner of the living room to sober up. I didn't want to fall asleep in the middle of a party like at Thad's cousin's house. Once in the chair, I began to eat and looked around the room. They were all in their early and mid-twenties. Some were huddled into a corner talking about their love lives or something, and others were scattered into twos, engaging in conversation I was too distracted to pay attention to. This was different from the party Thad and I crashed. There wasn't garbage littered everywhere, or people crawling across the floor in their intoxication. These women were mature. They understood that you could have fun without making a mess of yourself.

These are my kind of people, I thought as I observed everyone.

"All right. Étienne. Let's hear about your Thursday night." Rhonda silenced the whole room, forcing all eyes on me. This *was* the reason she invited me over in the first place. She was too impatient to wait for our next shift together.

I felt like a deer caught in the path of those ridiculously bright, new LED headlights. I didn't know what to do. I froze as a wall of fear appeared in front of me. And I think she knew it caught me off guard as her eyes darted across the room, then landed on me again.

"Honey. It's okay. You're okay around us," she tried comforting me before adding, "Every one of us has one of you. And some, more." I wasn't sure what she meant by that at the time, though I do now.

"Wow. Um. This is weird." I gulped, then began. "So, um. I have this friend. Well, more than a friend now. I guess." I stopped for a second, heart pounding through my chest. "He's this guy in my grade who I've noticed for a long time. But not in a creepy way."

I gave them all a quick recap of Thad and how we met on the last day of school. Then I told them about our time spent together leading up to the night of his birthday. I couldn't believe how comfortable I felt around these women. Was it the alcohol helping me talk? Or was it their presence? They all gave me their undivided attention. They welcomed me into their lives and were genuinely interested in who I was. So why would I hide from them? Why would I hide from you? You're the one who decided to read this.

Rhonda walked over to me and handed me a rocks glass that was filled to the brim. I probably didn't need more alcohol, but I guess they would take care of me if I had too much. I stopped for a minute and looked around the room, hesitant to continue speaking. She said it was a whisky sour and that I would enjoy it. I took a sip of the drink, being careful not to spill it, and felt the skin on my arms raise into goose bumps. I took another sip to see if it would help calm my nerves, which I think it did. Rhonda pulled a chair up and threw her arm around me, then I began describing exactly what happened after my night at the bar with Thad on Thursday. Well, Friday morning.

"So. We were driving home. I was still kind of upset with him and what he said about the almost-fight. His hand was in my lap, holding on to mine..."

18

THAD'S BIRTHDAY CONTINUED

"You okay?" he asked after seeing I was obviously still a little upset.

"I'm fine." I was trying to be, at least.

"Where are you going?" demanded Thad as we passed my street.

"What do you mean? I'm taking you home."

Did he want to go somewhere else? Sure, it was only one in the morning. But everyone in my house would have been asleep. And my mom had to work the next morning. If she had fallen asleep on the couch, the creak from the side door would definitely alarm her to my presence if I came in any later.

His eyes looked back and forth as he squeezed my hand, the anxiety pushing through his blank stare. "Could I maybe stay with you tonight?"

Could you stay with me? My back tightened. I didn't know what to say. Yes, of course I wanted him to stay over. And no. No. There would be too many questions posed by my family. I'd never had a guy friend stay over, not to mention someone I was falling for. And now that my mom knew, it was out of the question. Where was he going to stay? We had a spare room in the basement, but I wasn't going to throw him down there. It was like a dungeon. Maybe he could stay in my room with the door closed, and I'd sleep on the couch. I'd fallen asleep there countless times. Nobody would question finding me on the couch.

"Um. I..." I began, pulling my hand away from him to grab the wheel.

"I'm sorry," he said, cutting me off. "It's just that my dad has been blowing up my phone the entire night. Maybe he needs some time to chill before I go home."

"Yeah. That's probably a good idea."

Instead of pulling into the driveway and potentially waking my mom, I turned the headlights off and parked on the street in front of my neighbor's house. I told Thad not to exit the car himself since he was still drunk and a little clumsy. I got out first and closed my door as silently as I possibly could, then did the same on the passenger side as I held on to Thad. He wasn't really that drunk, but his body felt right leaning against mine. And I think he liked it too since he kept his arm around me.

We were able to sneak in through the side door unnoticed. Then took our shoes off and tried our hardest to remain inaudible as we climbed up the two steps to the kitchen.

"Shit," I whispered.

"Ooh look..." Callum began to speak, but I reached my free hand out to stop him from continuing.

"Shut up. You're going to wake Ma," I whispered into his ear, then pulled my hand off his face. "What are you doing?"

"I was getting some water. Sheesh. What are *you* doing?"

"None of your business. Go back to bed."

"None of my business, eh? Ten bucks and I wasn't here." He held out his hand.

Callum was the mischievous one of the twins and had been slowly turning into an opportunist. He was learning how to handle himself, which perplexed me since he was only ten years old. Niall was still naive and took everything at face value.

"I'll give it to you in the morning," I said. I didn't have any cash on me and didn't have the time to run to my room and grab money from the stash in my sock drawer.

"Fine. Fifteen then. Night, Thad." He waved and exited the kitchen with his water.

That son of a...

"I like him," whispered Thad as we tiptoed through the kitchen.

"Take him then." I shook my head.

I slowly closed my bedroom door to try to minimize the squeaky noise that normally resonated from the hinges. I wouldn't have given any thought to this on a normal night. I would have even left the light on and my door cracked open if I wanted to stay up on my laptop. This time was different. This time I needed my privacy and I needed to make sure no one else woke up.

Once the door was closed, I placed a large book in front of it so it would stay closed, then turned to see Thad sitting on my bed. He motioned me to come sit next to him, patting the covers. I stood motionless, watching him watch me, my mind spinning and trying to think of how to handle the morning and what would happen, depending on who was home when I woke up.

I sat on the edge of the bed with my legs crossed. I couldn't believe we were on my bed, in the middle of the night. This time I made the first move. I placed my hand on his upper leg, which he flexed as I gazed into his eyes. I'd never wanted to be next to someone more in my life. I wanted to kiss him. I wanted him to put his arms around me and lay me down on the bed. I wanted to feel the weight of his body on top of mine. Is that too much detail?

My heart was racing, pumping adrenaline through my veins. I felt more out of breath sitting with him than I would have felt running a 5k cross country race. He was perfectly still, staring into my eyes as he smiled. He seemed so relaxed. Had he done this before? Who hadn't by the time they were seventeen? Well, I hadn't. But I was determined to change that. He put his arm around me and pulled me in further, so the tip of his nose was touching mine.

"Eskimo kiss." He chuckled, his breath warming my face.

"Eski what?" I pulled away. I'd never in my life heard those two words together.

He rolled his eyes then pulled me toward him, locking me in with both of his arms. "You're so weird. Come here."

He rubbed the tip of his nose against mine again, sending an electric current through my body. I put my arm around him and pulled his body closer to me, then uncrossed my left leg and moved it to the side so our torsos were mere inches apart. He closed his eyes, then I closed mine. And he moved in first, tilting his head until his lips were firmly locked with mine.

It only lasted for a moment, but it was a moment that would last a lifetime in my memory. I opened my eyes and looked down to see him smiling. He nudged my chin to look up into his icy blue eyes, then put his arms around me once more and we slowly collapsed into the bed.

This was my very first kiss. I couldn't have imagined it to be as perfect as it was. We elongated our bodies onto the bed and faced each other. He grabbed my hip, and I felt more aroused than I ever had before. He finally confirmed what I was suspecting: He liked me, and he wanted me. I slid my arm under him and started to pull him in closer. I wanted my lips to caress his again.

"Shit," I whispered. We were interrupted by a scratching noise coming from the bottom of my bedroom door.

"Is that Frankie?" He popped his head up.

It was my faithful companion Frankie coming to check on me. The best moment in my life had to be interrupted by my little best friend. And I bet you he did it on purpose. Frankie could always tell when I was happy, sad, angry, or even bored. He always came to check up on me when I was alone and in need. I was in need this time, but I was not alone. And I needed something else. Someone else.

I cracked the door open, and he waddled in, panting as if he'd been running around the house all night. Then I closed the door and placed books on the floor in front of it. I turned and Frankie jumped up into the spot where I was, next to Thad.

"So um. I've got some shorts and a T-shirt you could use. That way you don't have to sleep in jeans," I said, pulling out some clothes for myself. I normally slept in my underwear and a T-shirt, but I wasn't sure how this was supposed to work.

"It's all right. I sleep in my underwear." He smiled as he rubbed Frankie's belly.

"Oh. Um. Okay." I hesitated then kicked the book to the side to open the door, carrying my sleeping clothes.

"Where are you going?" he whispered.

"I uhh. I was going to sleep on the couch. You can have my bed. But make sure to move the book back so the door doesn't slip open."

"Do you...are you okay? Was *that* okay?" He pointed to where we had been lying.

Of course it was okay.

"No yeah. I..." I grinned. "I thought you might want some privacy."

"You're hilarious. Close the door. I'll sleep on the floor."

"No. Take my bed. You're the guest. I'll sleep on the floor."

We could have slept in the bed together. We fell asleep next to each other on the beanbags at the party. But that was an accident, I thought. And sleeping in my bed with another guy wouldn't look right if one of the twins barged into the room, as they often did.

I took off my jeans then changed my shirt. I decided not to change my underwear. I was not ready for someone to see me change like that. He had seen me change my bathing suit, but that was different. Normally I'd go to bed in clean underwear. I usually changed my underwear at least twice a day. Yes, I know I'm extra.

I grabbed a blanket from the closet after changing my shirt and Thad handed me one of the several pillows that decorated my bed. I sat upright on the floor then leaned my head back to rest on the nightstand. I turned to the left to admire the person with whom I shared such a wonderful moment, but Frankie sprang up and extended his long body and neck to lick my face. He licked my nose, then my ear for a second before I gently pushed him to the side to make eye contact with Thad. Thad stood up, pulled down his fitted jeans and threw them to the side, then pulled off his shirt and threw it next to the jeans lying on the floor. I would have at least folded them if I were him—which I ended up doing after he sat back down on my bed.

"You're hilarious. You don't have to do that."

"I do, though. Or else I'll be awake tonight thinking about it sitting there on the floor. Disheveled."

He stood, holding in a laugh as I placed his folded clothes on top of my dresser. I would not have guessed he was the type of guy to be sporting contoured briefs. It was hot.

He grabbed ahold of my waist and pulled me close to him. The heat from his skin seeped through my shirt, warming me as I tried my hardest to calm my excitement. *This is not the time, Étienne.* I put my arms around him. We kissed again. One last glorious—and might I say sensual—kiss before we retired for the night.

The sound of thumping woke me the next morning as my brothers were running throughout the house. My mom must have already left for work; she would have been screaming at them if she were home. I opened my eyes and blinked several times so my vision could focus. I know I shouldn't have, but I slept in my contacts again for fear of waking someone while washing my hands in the bathroom.

Thad was leaning so far off the bed I thought he was going to fall on me. I looked down at his extended arm and saw he was holding on to my hand. *Wait. What?* I looked again. I did not remember feeling him reach down for me while we were sleeping. I carefully unlocked his hand from mine and got up. He wasn't just leaning over the edge to hold my hand; he was forced to sleep that way. Frankie claimed his spot right behind Thad. He did that to me sometimes. Actually, all the time.

I remember one night being violently awoken when I was fifteen. Frankie had fallen asleep on the pillow next to my face, after I was already asleep. I rolled over, nearly crushing him. He attacked out of fear, biting my left ear so hard he almost pierced it. It hurt like hell, but I couldn't be mad at him. It was my fault.

I sneaked out of my room without waking him and ran to the kitchen to make some toast and jelly for Thad, and to bring him an orange juice.

"Where's Riley?" I asked Callum who was sitting at the kitchen table watching TV.

"Mom dropped her off at Ashley's this morning. They're going to Metro Park for the day."

You wouldn't understand how quickly my muscles relaxed, releasing my anticipated stress. Riley and I had cleared the air, but it was still a relief for her not to be there to witness me and Thad.

"Where's Niall?" I asked. I thought I'd heard him before leaving my room.

"In the back setting up the Wii. You know you still owe me for last night."

"Yeah, yeah. Can you guys stay in there for a little?" I pointed toward the rear living room.

"Another five bucks." He winked then turned away.

Little shit. At least I knew he'd keep his mouth shut.

As I was carrying what little I had to offer Thad, Frankie came running through the sitting room. I must not have closed the door properly. I turned the corner and peaked through the crack in the door before entering. Thad was standing in his underwear, looking through his phone with his right hand as he shuffled his hair with the other.

"Oh." He jumped as I opened the door, probably thinking it was someone else.

"It's just me. Sorry." I set the plate and glass on top of my dresser. "I'm not sure what you like."

"That's perfect." He leaned forward and gave me a peck square on the lips.

Please do it again. Bring your lips over here.

"Hey. I don't have to work until later today. Want to do something maybe?" I asked as he was throwing on his clothes.

"I can't. We're all going to visit a school my sister's interested in."

"Oh. Then let me grab your shoes." I opened the door and ran to the hall that connected the kitchen to the side door.

"Hey. Can I tell you something?" he asked after I returned from the door with his shoes.

"Of course," I said.

"I. Um. I don't really know how to say this. I think. I really like you." He grinned. "You just...you make me feel good," he added, sending butterflies through my stomach.

You could have flown me to the moon and back and I don't think I would have been as excited as I was. He finally put it into words. I finally had vocal affirmation that he thought of me the way I thought of him.

"I just..." He sat on my bed and tucked his face into his arms. "I don't know what to think."

My stomach ascended into my chest as if I had been thrown into the abyss. Was he confused? Had he never had feelings like this for another guy? I don't think he was ready for this.

"I don't know how to tell people about this. Or who I could say it to."

We both knew his parents were not an option. They would need a lot of time before he could say anything. But why was he so afraid to mention anything to his friends? Most people our age didn't care as much anymore. I remember the year previous when we had to debate Don't Ask Don't Tell in a government class. Now that I look back, our teacher brought that up for a reason—he was in the military before becoming a teacher. And I definitely remember seeing him, or someone who looked like him, once in a gay club after graduating high school. Anyway, it heartened me that so many of my peers thought it was dumb to discriminate against LGBTQ soldiers.

"Would it really be that hard?" I sat next to him and put my hand on his leg.

"Yes. It would. Don't push me, Étienne." He grunted, holding his hands together. This subject was touchy. But I didn't think it was this sensitive of a subject.

Étienne, stop. You're not even out to your friends yet. "Hey. It's totally fine. We don't have to say anything to anyone. I'm sorry."

"That's not fair though. Is it?" He rested his head on my shoulder and looked up at me.

He was conflicted about the situation. He wanted to be with me, but he didn't know how to. I didn't really know how either. But I definitely thought it would have been easier for me than him. For starters, my dad was gone. My mom and Riley wouldn't have cared. They'd always dropped hints, insisting gay people should be treated as anyone else. It would have been easy to tell my brothers. They were both so young I could have introduced anyone as my boyfriend, and they would have shrugged and asked me to take them out for ice cream.

"How do you think your sister would react?" I asked.

"I don't know. Maybe she'd be fine."

"Like I said. You don't have to say anything. But I think it might make you feel better about it if you did have someone you could tell," I said. "I haven't told any of my friends either. Except one person."

I explained that I had one person—just one—who I could talk to about this and who I knew didn't judge me. It was my coworker, Rhonda. She was so far enough removed from my life that whoever she spoke with wouldn't have known me.

"She seems cool." He grinned.

"She is."

Thad slipped on his shoes. And then pulled me in for a tight hug, which he desperately needed. We held on to each other for a while. Much longer than a normal hug. Like that time in the pool when I needed him. This time, he needed me. And I wanted to hold on as long as I could for him.

"Hey," I began before he reached the sidewalk.

He looked up. I winked. And his pale cheeks blushed.

SUNDAY 15 JUNE 2008

19

WHAT DID I SAY?

I didn't expect to drink as much as I had during Rhonda's gathering. The vibration coming from my phone woke me up earlier than I would have liked. Only parts of the night were present in my memory after revealing what had happened the night of Thad's birthday. I do remember Rhonda handing me another drink, and then her friend Kate made me take a shot of something, which was my tipping point. I woke up in Rhonda's spare bedroom. My clothes were folded and put away. And I was by myself.

I pulled my phone out from under the pillow, wondering why it was there since I always keep it on my nightstand. The spare bedroom had a nightstand as well. Maybe I wanted it to be close in case. In case of what? I'm not going there. Then I grabbed my glasses, which *were* on the side table.

I flipped my screen open and saw a message from Thad. *Are you alright?* the message read.

I looked around the room again to make sure I hadn't done anything, but it looked tidier than when I first dropped my bag next to the bed the day before. *Wait. Did I call him last night?* I checked my call history. *You idiot.* I called him at three in the morning. *Shit. I hope I didn't make a fool of myself.* I really hoped I hadn't. Thad was already feeling uncertain about our relationship. And if I jeopardized that, I'd hate myself for it.

"Hey," I whispered through the phone. I wasn't sure if Rhonda was awake yet.

"Hey. Are you all right this morning?"

"What do you mean? I, ah. I don't remember calling you last night. What happened?" I asked.

"Well. You called me really late to tell me you wanted to kiss my face." He laughed before adding, "Then you started falling asleep on the line as you were confessing your love for me."

My heart began to thump loud enough to wake the entire neighborhood. What had I done? Yes, I felt that way. But I was definitely not ready to say it out loud, especially not to him. This could have pushed him away. *You're an idiot, Étienne. You blew it.* I felt my anxieties materializing within a short distance of my vision. *This shouldn't have happened. I should have stayed home and kept quiet.*

"Do you really feel that way?" he asked. He already guessed the answer from my silence. "You do then."

"Thad I...I'm sorry. It wasn't supposed to come out like that. This is going too fast. I'm stupid."

"Hey. Relax. It's...it's a bit sudden. But..." He paused before adding, "It's okay."

"This is so embarrassing. I'm never drinking again." I hit the pillow next to me.

"Étienne. You're all right. Tell me about the night?" He changed the subject.

I gave him a recap of my night and talked about all the people Rhonda knew. Though I left out the part of me telling everyone about him. And about our relationship. I didn't want to worry him more. I was really attracted to this person. Not just physically attracted. Something clicked between us. Imagine observing someone from afar for years, then finding out they liked you too. It had to mean something more. Right?

"Want to maybe hang out today?" I asked. I wanted to see him. We hadn't seen each other since early Friday morning.

"Can't really go out right now. My parents are pissed I didn't come home Thursday night." He sighed before adding, "Plus, my dad's being weird around me. Not sure why."

Thad said I probably should go home and relax since I had ingested so much booze the night before, which was a good idea. I got up from the bed and sneaked into the bathroom with my bag to get ready for the day. From what I could see past the hallway as I entered the bathroom, the living room looked cleaned up. *Is Rhonda awake?*

Yes. She left a towel for me. I didn't want to have to ask her for a towel since I wasn't sure if she was still sleeping.

Once inside, I positioned myself directly under the shower head for a few minutes. I'd hoped the steamy water would help with my headache, but it didn't. The only thing that helped relieve the stinging in my frontal lobe was when I put in my cold contact lenses. They had been sitting overnight in the pocket of my bag not far from the vent on the floor, being blasted with cool air.

"Hey. Want a coffee?" Rhonda pointed to the pot on her counter as I entered the kitchen.

"I'm good. Thank you though. What happened last night?" I asked, embarrassed.

"Oh nothing. You were being cute. Kate and I shouldn't have forced you to drink. You're still only a teenager." She laughed.

"Are you sure I was okay? Did I embarrass myself? Or anyone else?" I wanted to know. I needed to know. I didn't want to be out in public and run into someone who was at the party and not know I had done something wrong. Or worse, I didn't want to one day stumble upon embarrassing photos of me.

"Étienne, chill. You were fine. You even helped Kate and me clean everything before passing out." She shook her head, rolling her eyes.

Yeah, that sounds like me.

"Why don't we go out for breakfast." She stood up from the stool beside the kitchen peninsula.

"I don't think I can eat anything. I've got this pinching in the pit of my stomach. It wasn't there when I woke up." I massaged my abdomen.

"All right then. I'll get ready and take you home. But remember for next time, you need to drink a bunch of water before going to bed. It really helps the next morning."

Will there be a next time?

"Thank you." I smiled.

I probably should have taken Rhonda's offer for breakfast. When she dropped me off at home everyone was there in the kitchen, including Laura and my grandma. They were all waiting as I entered the house. My mom asked how my night was. I didn't give her much detail but explained that everyone loved the hummus and pita sandwiches I made. Laura asked if I had any alcohol to drink, winking as she plunged her hand into her purse. Probably looking for a cigarette. I told them I did but had very little, a truth my grandma was not pleased with.

"You mean to tell me you let him stay the night at an older woman's house? And he had *alcohol*?" She sneered at my mom.

She side-eyed my grandma. "*Mom.* We've talked about this."

Talked about what? I examined the two of them. What had they been talking about? Me?

It was me who went, though. And I knew my grandma wouldn't be mad at me. In her mind when a minor did something bad or stupid, it was the parents' fault for not anticipating and stepping in before the trouble arose. It was amusing when she would heckle my mom, though. Maybe that's what they talked about—my grandma reprimanding her in front of her children.

My family could have grilled me for hours, asking what I did that night and what exactly I had to drink. But again, I hated the attention.

Laura walked to the side door with her cigarette. My mom's and grandma's eyes were still locked in a psychic battle, so I quietly shuffled backward onto the sitting room carpet and then turned toward my bedroom.

"Who touched my room?" I yelled, holding on to the door-frame as I swung around and addressed everyone still in the kitchen. My bed had been unmade.

"It was Niall," Callum admitted.

Apparently, my mom thought it would be fine if Niall used my room since I wasn't home. The twins shared a room, whereas Riley and I had our own rooms. I threw down my stuff and began pacing. Not only was my bed messed up, now I had to change all of the bedding. Who knows what kind of dirt a ten-year-old boy brings in from outside?

"Étienne, calm down. He's your brother," my mom said, entering my room after I slammed the door.

"Ma. What are you doing? I'm taking my clothes off. I need to take a shower." I'd already taken one at Rhonda's, but I wanted to take another. I never feel as clean as I'd like until I'm in my own home.

"Hold on a second, Étienne. I haven't had the chance to talk to you." She closed the bedroom door.

Umm. What now?

What would she want to talk about? I didn't think I'd done anything wrong. She was fine with me staying at Rhonda's. I didn't get into any trouble. Frankie was sitting in his bed when I walked in, so he was fine. Did I miss something?

"When I left for work on Friday morning I saw another pair

of shoes at the back door." She stared right through me. "Your feet aren't that size."

Panic consumed my thoughts as I tried my hardest to keep a straight face. *You have to be kidding me. This is not happening right now.* How would I explain this to her? I was not ready for this. I'd never had anyone stay over for the night before, except Dana. And in that case my mom made me sleep in the basement bedroom so Dana could have my bed.

"Oh. My friend. He got in a fight with his dad. He just...he asked if he could stay over." I tried to play it off.

"In your room?" She tilted her head and rested her hands on her hips. She wasn't buying it.

"I slept on the floor with Frankie." I had to try to make it seem believable. Most of it was true, but I still don't think she believed me.

"Okay, we need to set some ground rules. You're more mature than the average seventeen-year-old. You have been for a long time. But you're still a kid," she began. "You can't just have someone stay the night without telling me. Don't do that again."

I was welcome to bring any friend home to meet her, she lectured. Which was her way of hinting that she wanted to meet this mysterious friend. My Saturday night with Rhonda would also be a one-time thing until after I turned eighteen. And if I wanted to drink, I needed to be at home. She would need to be there, and only one drink was allowed. I needed to be a little more responsible and more of a role model for my brothers.

I took a second shower and decided to hang around the house for the day. I started my laundry, which included the messy bedding. Mowed the lawn between my two loads of laundry. Then decided to take Frankie for a walk. Without my brothers. This needed to be a structured walk. No meandering and sniffing every object.

The walk gave me time to think and sort through my life without the constant interruptions from home. I knew I had been going out and spending a lot of time away from my family, but was I really a bad example to my brothers? What was I to do with them other than reprimand them when they were being silly? They were several years younger than me and we didn't really have anything in common. We barely looked like siblings. They liked soccer while I liked swimming and running. It wasn't that I didn't like them. We had different interests, and rightfully so. They were ten, going on eleven, and I was seventeen.

The sound of a car engine approached from behind Frankie and me. But it was moving too slow to be someone passing by. We were about to turn the corner of my street when I heard, "Hey."

"I thought you couldn't leave the house today," I said after turning around.

Thad grinned. "My parents went to a casino downtown."

"Park. Come walk with us for a little." I gestured him to follow.

This morning felt weird, and I think I may have scared him during my drunken confession late in the night. He looked like he had something on his mind, and he hesitated to stop the car. But Frankie barked in his direction, which I think encouraged him to oblige. Frankie really was a great wingman. Wherever I took him during a walk, he attracted a crowd.

Thad parked his car a house before the stop sign at the end of my street and joined us as I turned right. We were near the entrance of the high school parking lot, and we turned into the lot so we could walk along the tall fencing. There wouldn't be anyone around and we would have the privacy to speak openly.

"Do you recall the first time we ever spoke?" I asked, tapping his hand with my pinky.

"You mean like two weeks ago? Right?"

"It was in the fifth grade."

"How can you remember that?"

"I remember everything," I said. I do remember everything.

It's a blessing and a curse. I have photographic memory, which has always helped me in school. I also usually don't forget where things are. Unfortunately, I remember every bad thing anyone has ever said to me, and even when and where they said it. I can forgive, but I can never forget.

"Okay. Go on." He waved. I now had his full attention.

In elementary, my school hosted D.A.R.E. classes to teach kids about substance abuse and violence. You'd think fifth grade was a bit too young to address such a subject, but I assure you it wasn't. I've known plenty of people in high school and beyond who needed those assemblies when they were younger. It's scary to see someone you love falling into that. Sometimes it isn't even their choice.

Our class had been visited weekly by a representative for most of the year. We learned about substance abuse and how to reach out for help. We learned about physical abuse within the family unit. And all of this, all these weekly meetings, led to a grand D.A.R.E. assembly hosted in the school auditorium with all of our parents about a month before the year ended, on a Friday night. Before the event, our class was tasked with decorating our black D.A.R.E. T-shirts and writing letters to our future selves promising that we'd try to resist drugs and avoid violence. A few people in our class volunteered to read theirs out loud to the entire auditorium.

On the way home from the assembly, my mom turned to me from the passenger's seat and said that she ran out of film in her camera and could only take a few photos. I shrugged. Who was I to really care about something like that? My family consisted of several people who were attached to their cameras and had thousands of photos developed each year. It wasn't a bother to have a few less of me in the pile. I thought my mom was finished, so I looked at her and shook my head, confused why she hadn't turned forward.

"This really nice dad was standing next to me and offered to take pictures of you. He's going to get them developed this weekend and his son will bring them to class on Monday. He's in your class." She smiled, exposing a red smudge of lipstick on her two front teeth.

"Ma. No. That's so embarrassing. Why would you do that?" I moaned.

"That's embarrassing? Sure, Étienne. Yeah, okay then." She rolled her eyes.

Monday came. I was in class and didn't know which of my classmates would be the person who'd bring the photos. I spent the morning daydreaming of learning how to fly so I could escape the confines of my school. It wasn't until after lunch when we were heading past our lockers to go out onto the playground that I heard his voice call my name. His hair was even fairer than it was when we reintroduced ourselves years later.

"Yeah. I have to give you these." He handed me a sealed Ziploc bag with some twenty photos of me in it. His right arm was stretched out, his left behind his back. He must have been as mortified as I was. Imagine having to carry around a clear package with photos of some other boy in the fifth grade. I would have died if it were in reverse.

"Thanks." I half smiled.

We both walked away, never to speak again until our last day of junior year.

"You're kidding?" he blurted. "I think I remember that."

"Yup. That was the first and only time we've ever really spoken to each other before this summer." I bit my lip as our eyes met.

We had walked through the alley between the school and my street and reached the bleachers of the track and football field. The gate wasn't locked, so we decided to go in and sit. Frankie needed a rest anyway.

"I heard about your friend's party the other day. Did you

go?" His left hand grabbed my right, and they rested on the bleacher between us.

"Nah. I wasn't really invited," I admitted.

"You what? Why?" he demanded.

"It's nothing. We're not really in a good place right now. How did you hear about it?"

"Supposedly everyone was there. I heard it got out of hand," he said.

Dana not inviting me bothered me at first, but we were in a rocky place and I thought that maybe she needed space. But Thad bringing it up made me realize that I was absolutely not over it. She was my best friend, and she chose not to invite me to what I guess was the party of the year. Had those people actually been my real friends? They'd forgotten to invite me several times over sophomore and junior year. And then this.

"So, my dad had a talk with me after our phone call this morning." He looked away before adding, "Well, more of a yell and a threat." He took a more serious tone.

A threat? What happened? I straightened up, looking into his eyes.

"He saw me on Thursday night. He saw me getting into your car. And he saw me kiss your cheek."

"What'd he say?"

I didn't think his face could have gotten any whiter than it was, but it did. It looked like the life was being flushed out of him. "He made me swear I would never do it again." Thad inhaled deeply. "He said he would send me away to some camp if this went any further. If I continued to be like this." He lifted his head for a moment, revealing his red eyes, swollen with tears.

My mind went blank as he spoke. I wanted to comfort him. I wanted to say something to ease his fear but I didn't know how to put the words together. Maybe my arm around his shoulder would have helped. I dared not to, though. He seemed too on edge as he recounted the interaction with his dad. How could his dad say something like that? My dad wasn't an easy walk through the park either, but at least he never threatened to send me away.

"I don't know what to do." He leaned forward, head between his knees, and unlocked our grip. Sniffling periodically to try to hold in the tears.

I scooched closer to him and leaned onto his side with my arm around his back. I held on to him. He needed to know I was there for him. Frankie moved from where he had been sprawled out and nudged Thad's left shin. Thad snorted, trying to cover his half cry, half laugh.

"I'm so confused, Étienne. I'm sorry to put this on you. I don't know how we can..." He lifted his head to continue, but I stopped him before he could finish.

"It's okay. We don't have to think about that right now."

He didn't have to, but I was thinking about it.

MONDAY 16 JUNE 2008

20

LIKE OLD TIMES

"Hun. Hey. What's on your mind?" Rhonda asked, peeking through the doorway of the back room. I was on the floor sorting through molds again; there were only two boxes left. But I'm sure Jason would have found more somewhere above the ceiling tiles for me to sort through when he had the time. He was good at pulling stuff out of thin air.

I hadn't been able to concentrate all morning at work. The thought of what Thad said the day before weighed heavily on my mind. I lay on my bed awake all night as my thoughts circled endlessly. What was I going to do? For the first time in my life, I found someone who liked me for me. What was he going to do? He couldn't exist as himself in his own house.

"Hey. You with the face." She stepped forward and tapped my shoulder.

I looked up and tried to force a grin. I really wasn't in the mood to speak to anyone. I had barely spoken to my mom in the car that morning. Luckily, Jason only came in for a moment before leaving, giving me enough space to breathe. I think I would have had to walk out if he were there pestering me about my hair or the way I sit cross-legged on the floor.

"Hey. Take the floor. I need to do something back here," she said to the main jeweler.

She grabbed my arm, yanked me from the floor, and pulled up both jewelers' rolling chairs. It was a slow day and the jeweler's counterpart decided to leave early. I sat in one of the chairs while she ran to the kitchen for something.

"What are you doing?" I asked. She was carrying two glasses of wine. "Rhonda, we're at work. I don't want to drink."

"Oh who cares. Jason lets us drink a glass every day during the holiday season. Plus, he's not here and the back-room cameras were disconnected until our new computer comes in. Actually, when *are* those coming in?" She looked up at the corner of the room where a camera hovered over us.

She handed me a glass and took a sip of her drink, then I followed suit. I know what you're thinking. Yes, I was too young to be drinking. Yes, I had been drinking more than I should have. But I promise you I was being responsible.

"Spill," she demanded.

I recounted Thad's conversation with me from Sunday afternoon and how he had been feeling confused and asked to have some time to himself. Yes. After I leaned into him, telling him we didn't have to worry about it, that we could take it slow, he asked if I would give him a little space to think. He was confused. He'd never liked a guy before me. He didn't know how his friends would react, and he didn't know what to do about his parents.

She leaned in and wrapped her arm around me. "That really sucks, Étienne."

"I don't know what to do," I whispered.

"Let him have some space. Don't push him. It could make things worse."

We sat in the back room for a while. She finished her glass before returning to the floor. I only took another sip then went into the kitchen cupboard to make myself a relaxing chamomile tea. It did help in letting me relax a little, which encouraged me to organize an entire box filled with hundreds of old single-use molds.

My mom noted my mood change on the way home from picking me up. "How was work today?"

"It was fine. I got a lot done and Jason wasn't there to pile on the work."

I did feel better. All I needed when I was feeling down, or when I was in a pickle, was to have someone who would listen to me. My head was clearer. I knew, or at least hoped, that things would get better, and that Thad and I would move past this obstacle.

"What do you say we go to Greektown tonight for dinner? Like old times," my mom proposed.

"Sounds like a plan," I replied.

Greektown is a small area of downtown Detroit filled with restaurants surrounding one of the three casinos. Throughout my childhood, we'd dine out as a family every Sunday after-noon. Normally we'd pick one of the several restaurants near the Nautical Mile, but on special occasions we'd drive down as a family to Greektown so my dad could run into the casino and gamble a bit while we waited for our orders. My mom and her friends would also go there a few times a year for a night out.

Once home, my mom ordered us all to change our clothes and to put on something less casual. Where we were going wasn't the type of place you needed to dress up for, but my mom wanted to make an occasion of it. It was easy for me since I didn't really own anything too casual, compared to Riley and the twins who loved dressing comfortably. Though Riley had been making more of an effort after she and Nate started dating.

"You're driving. I'm going to have a drink." My mom threw the keys to me as I closed the dog gate to the rear living room.

"See ya later, little man." I waved to Frankie as everyone exited the side door.

"Argh. Callum! You idiot," Riley yelled after I heard a hard thump. We'd barely left the driveway.

Both of my brothers decided it would be a good idea to bring one Nintendo DS to share. Both had one, so I don't understand why they left the other at home. They fought over it after Niall decided to restart a session after losing a game, then Callum grabbed it and threw it against the window, causing it to bounce back and ram Riley in the forehead. She screamed at them before my mom had the chance to, then chucked it behind her and into the trunk. My sister wasn't above destroying your property if you angered her.

Trust me, never get in Riley's way. I was the one who faced the wrath of her very first explosion when we were much younger. She threw a snow globe at me once during a Christmas party. It missed my face by a few hairs and shattered into the wall behind me.

"Étienne. Hold your brothers' hands." My mom pointed to the three of us as we exited the car.

"Ma, why? They're fine." I stepped back, watching Riley chuckle.

She glared at my sister. "You think it's funny?"

"I mean come on. They're not babies. They can follow behind us," said Riley, hand rested on her hip.

"No. It's a few blocks away and we're downtown. Niall, grab Étienne's hand. And Callum, grab Riley's."

I know my mom still thought of the twins as little kids, which they technically were. But was it really necessary to hold their hands to the restaurant?

As we turned the corner onto Monroe, I looked up at the massive shiny blue skyscraper sticking out like an awkward-looking shard of glass on the far end of the neighborhood. This new thing dwarfed all the restaurants and businesses bordering the narrow street. It blocked much of the view of the sky, almost ruining the twinkling strings of lights that crisscrossed the street.

I hadn't really seen it up close since it began construction. It seemed like something my dad would have wanted to see since he liked this area so much. Outings as a family had become few and far between.

Niall loosened his grip when we approached the restaurant entrance, and revulsion kicked into my throat. "Eww." I looked at my hand. *Why is his hand sticky?*

"Do you remember when you brought Liz and me down in the middle of the night?" my mom asked. We had just been seated at the restaurant and were waiting to place our order.

"I do. I passed my test for segment one and got my learner's permit," I responded, admiring the happiness on my mom's face.

Riley put down her buttered bread. "When was this? Why wasn't I there?"

"You wanted nothing to do with us that night, Riley." I pointed my butter knife in her direction.

My mom had one of her closest friends Liz stay over for the night. She lived several hours away and only visited a few times each year. My mom invited several of her friends over for drinks. My dad kept the twins busy in the basement, leaving my mom some space. He may have been hardheaded, but he loved my mom. Riley stayed in her room all night; she went through a short phase of not wanting to be near anyone. I on the other hand loved hanging out with my mom's friends. I helped with the setup. I listened in on all their conversations and gossip. Then I helped clean and put everything away at the end of the night.

All my mom's friends cleared out by midnight, save Liz. Her and my mom weren't quite ready to retire. The two of them wanted to continue the night and asked if I wanted to practice my nighttime driving to get some extra hours into my driving log. I was more than happy to and drove them in the middle of the night. They picked Greektown since most of the restaurants and bars closed really late thanks to the casino. We ended up at this same restaurant. I ordered a spanakotiropita and a Pepsi, and my mom and Liz ordered a flaming saganaki with their cocktails. We'd laughed and talked so much, the waitstaff started giving us dirty looks when the restaurant finally emptied for the night.

"What a fun night." She shook her head.

"It was," I said, handing Niall a napkin after noticing bread-crumbs accumulating on his lap next to me.

I felt somewhat at ease sitting there with her talking about times past. Like the stresses of the last year and a half of our lives were finally starting to fade. The only thing that would have made this moment better was if *he* had texted me.

WEDNESDAY 18 JUNE 2008

21

DANA

I was sitting on the back porch watching the twins kick around the soccer ball this morning, thinking about when Thad would finally decide to talk to me.

He hadn't reached out to me since our conversation in the bleachers on Sunday. Nor did I hear from him Monday night after dinner downtown with my family. I spent most of that night and the following day asking myself if I should reach out to him, then decided not to for fear that it would drive him further into his own chagrin. A thought appeared in my head late in the day on Tuesday while I was lying in Riley's hammock looking up at the night sky.

"What if he's thinking the same? What if he wants to talk to me, but doesn't know what to say?" I asked myself, looking for the moon through the faint sliver of clouds.

I put together a message to text him but found it hard to press send without Rhonda's voice overpowering my thoughts. I regretted erasing the message and listening to Rhonda's advice. I wanted to talk to him. I needed to talk to him. But he needed more time to sort things out. It couldn't have been easy with both of his parents being as closed minded as they were. I wondered though, did his mom really feel that way? Or was she falling in line with what his dad was saying? That was a valid question. From what I've heard, moms usually tend to be more accepting with their sons. Usually, but I guess not always.

As I watched my twin brothers argue whether or not Callum actually kicked the ball into the goal at the other end of the yard, around the corner near the front gate Frankie started barking at a dog and its owner passing by. And as I got up to go grab him, my phone vibrated. I inhaled, hoping it was finally a message from Thad. I reached down and grabbed my phone, then let out a disappointed, "Oh."

Hey, Dana texted.

Should I reply? I wondered. My fingers hovered over the keyboard for a minute before typing, *Hi Dana.*

Are you at work today?

"She wants to hang out. Maybe this is a good step. We'll fix this wedge between us," I said under my breath.

No. Sitting in the backyard with the twins.

Maybe want to come over? she texted.

Come here instead? I asked, hoping she'd say yes.

I was not about to go to her house and be ambushed. I also didn't want to pretend like everything was fine in front of her mom. She was a considerate person, and I didn't want her in this mess. She would only have burdened herself with trying to bring us back together like that time in eighth grade when Dana was more interested in me than I was in her and wanted to be boyfriend and girlfriend. I shut that down as quickly as possible, using the excuse that she was like a sister to avoid telling her I wasn't interested in girls. Her mom probably understood the situation better than she had, using her charm to get us back to being friends.

Never mind. Forget it, the message said. I imagined her dropping her phone on her bed and rolling her eyes as she wrote this last message, her hair probably a new color again.

Wait. Why don't we go for ice cream? Hopefully this was a better compromise.

K. Be there in an hour.

Alrighty, I replied, worrying about the *K* response.

The ice cream shop was the perfect place. It was public, but we could also sit on the bench in the back of the patio where no one else would hear us.

Callum and Niall asked if they could come with me. I told them that it was only Wednesday, and that they'd already gone twice this week. I didn't want them there distracting Dana and me like the last time. They would have been a good buffer between us, but we needed an actual discussion if we were going to clear the air. And this time, I would tell her everything about Thad and me. I was cautious the last time we spoke, for Thad's sake. But she wasn't a blabbermouth. And I always trusted her before this mess happened.

Dana wasn't there when I arrived, so I decided to order myself something and sit on the bench before anyone else tried to claim it. My usual order would have been a small chocolate and vanilla twist dipped in hard chocolate, but I decided to get a butterscotch milkshake, extra thick. It used to be my mom's favorite. When she would order it, she'd let me have a sip only if she could have the first bite of my cone. Which was fair. I only usually liked a sip of the milkshake, and she only liked the hard chocolate tip that folded over the swirl. A milkshake seemed like the better choice today since Dana and I would probably be there for a little while. And licking a melting ice cream cone while talking to someone seemed rude.

I waited another ten minutes past the time we had agreed on, nerves forcing me to slurp the milkshake, which gave me a brain freeze. I tried pushing my tongue against the roof of my mouth to alleviate the pain. Where was Dana?

Been here for a little while. You alright? I texted once the pain in my head subsided.

Another ten minutes went by with no response from her. So I decided to call her, worrying that maybe something had happened. No answer. Her voicemail didn't even pop up. *Why did she reject my call?*

There was still no response after a total of forty minutes waiting on the bench like a recluse. Yes, I waited that long. She was my best friend, what else was I going to do?

Not coming. Have fun with your little boyfriend, she texted before I was about to leave.

I stood, frozen in front of the bench. Only one thought came into my mind: *How did she find out?*

Dana, what are you talking about? I texted, power walking home, my veins pulsating as my heart rate thrummed, panic washing over me.

The phone vibrated again. *Don't try to deny it. People saw you at his house last week.*

People? Who? I had been a few houses away in the car. I still didn't understand how his dad saw us.

Great fucking friend, she wrote before I could respond.

I decided not to reply. When Dana was morose, only one person could calm her down. Sadly, she now hated the only person who could bring her back to herself. Replying or even trying to call would have made things worse. Eventually she would mellow, and we would be able to talk about it. The problem was, how did she find out? And how many other people knew about the two of us?

I tried calling Thad once I got home. I knew he wanted his space, but he needed to be warned. If Dana knew, then she found out from someone who wasn't at Thad's birthday. Which meant that others knew as well. And in our school, if a few people knew, the message was bound to spread like the STI outbreak among the senior class that year. This would scare him more than he already was. He would drift even further from me. Now that I knew the real Thad, I didn't think I could live a life without him. Too soon? Maybe. But that didn't matter to me. I only knew that I wanted him. I wanted him more than I cared to admit. He saw who I truly was, and he liked it.

I needed to figure out a way to fix this.

22

THAD

It only took me a few minutes to rush home, though it felt like an eternity. The little bits of happiness in my life were starting to unravel. My best friend ditched me after finding out I liked who I liked more than just a friend. Our friendship had already been stretched thin from the events of the past year, and now it was only hanging by a thread. I didn't know how long it would take for her to forgive me. If she ever would.

Then there was Thad. A guy I'd always had my eye on but stayed far enough away so he wouldn't notice. Then he noticed me for some reason. He was the first person to make me feel like I was allowed to be me. He needed his distance, but not answering my call threw me into a state of dismay.

At home, I lay on my bed staring at the uneven paint of the ceiling and trying not to let my thoughts pull me further into the abyss. The sound of my brothers running through the house didn't even bother me—I was too preoccupied with this tug-of-war between my best friend and my new boyfriend, if I could call him that. I did have one friend though, and I was relieved to hear the jingling sound of his collar as he waddled into my room and jumped up to see me. "Thanks mister," I said to him. He knew when I needed him.

What can I do? I need to talk to you.

I pushed myself upright on the bed and began to write another text message. But was a text message the most effective way to express my thoughts? It wasn't. A text couldn't possibly portray how I felt about Thad. I needed to do something more personal. Something that he could keep with him. I erased what I had written, for the second time, and grabbed one of my notebooks. I was going to write a letter to him. I wasn't going to send it in the mail, and I absolutely *was not* going to try to sneak up to his house. It would stay with me. I'd hold it on my person in case the chance to see him presented itself.

Dear Thad,

I wasn't sure how to put this into words when we last spoke. You deserve better than to have to hide in fear of what people might think of you. If people really knew who you were, if you would let people see the beautiful and kind person I've gotten to know, there'd be no reason for you to worry. The truth is, you're unlike any guy I've ever met. Actually, you're the only guy I can stand being around. When we're together, I can't stop myself from getting lost in your presence. The negative thoughts and stresses melt away. And I feel alive when I'm around you. You're one of the only people who has ever made me feel like I belong. And you give me a sense of pride in myself that I didn't know was there. I am forever grateful for knowing you.

You told me you needed some time to think about this, about your life and who you want to be. I understand. Please know that I'm here for you when you're ready.

Love,
Étienne

. . .

I ripped the letter out of the notebook I used to write my science fiction stories, cut off the frayed left side of the paper with the bathroom scissors since it wasn't a perforated notebook. Folded it several times. Then stuck it in my wallet. It felt more like a letter to me from me. I didn't know if I'd ever be able to give it to him. Maybe he'd never speak to me again. But someone needed to know how I felt.

If he never got to read it, at least you did.

THURSDAY 19 JUNE 2008

23

REJECTED

Yes, I thought to myself when I woke up. A delicious smell permeated the entire house. My mom decided to take the day off work and there was a full-spread Lebanese breakfast waiting for us in the kitchen. There were fluffy scrambled eggs, warm fooul moudammas, creamy labné with olive oil drizzled on top, zaatar manouche, and a platter with sliced cucumber, sliced tomato, cheese, mint leaves, and olives. Heaven!

This was the first time since my dad's death that the five of us had a sit-down breakfast together as a family. After his death, my mom threw herself into working more and picking up more patients so we could continue to afford living in our house.

"So. What do you guys want to do today?" my mom asked.

I shrugged and motioned my hands as if I didn't care. There wasn't anything I wanted to do. The only person I wanted to spend time with didn't want to talk to me. Or couldn't talk to me.

My sister's normal morning gloom brightened up. "Can we go to the mall?"

"Yeah, let's do that." Callum clapped then gave me the side

eye. He obviously wanted to spend the money he finagled from me.

"How about you two?" My mom pointed to Niall and me.

"Sure," we said in unison.

"Could we at least go to Somerset?" I suggested. My mom thankfully agreed.

I needed to be somewhere surrounded by beautiful things to distract me if I was going to be hauled with my entire family, staring at my phone waiting for the moment when Thad would be reaching out to me. And the Somerset Collection was the place to be when you felt low. It was only a half-hour drive from where I lived, but it was a completely different world. When I began clothing myself and stopped wearing the ill-fitted outfits my mom picked out for me, I'd take a little money out of each of my paychecks and get a few nice things from there about twice a year. I hadn't saved much to go shopping for this trip, but that didn't matter. My favorite part of this massive place was its colossal three-story atrium with its glass dome, illuminating the pools of water that surrounded the transparent elevators. If I didn't feel like shopping, or if I didn't have enough money to shop, I would sit on one of the atrium's many benches and watch people pass by.

Have you ever observed someone you didn't know and wondered what their life was like? How they were raised, how they came to be who they are now. It fascinates me. But I know other people might find it creepy.

There was one person who I had observed over the years. One person who made me ponder the same questions. Which, again, probably makes me seem like a creep. But I didn't think I was. I was curious about how other people lived. About how he lived. I used to watch him from afar and wondered what his life was like. How he came to be one of the more popular guys in school, yet still mysterious. And what he would be doing with his life after we graduated. It's not as exciting once you know.

For the most part, the people who passed by were normal people trying to survive in life like I was. Like I learned Thad was.

"Ma. I need some new bras and underwear," Riley declared as we passed Victoria's Secret.

"Yeah, you probably do." She grabbed one of her credit cards, pointed it to me, and said, "Here, Étienne. Take your brothers and let them both pick out a nice pair of shorts and a nice shirt."

Really, Ma. Can't I wander alone for a while?

"Nice pair of what? Do you not know who they are?" I said.

Riley and my mom entered the store, leaving me to look after my twin brothers. I mentioned a few places where I could help them find something as we headed toward the central atrium, but they didn't much care to pick out new clothes. They were the kind of boys who'd wear whatever their mom bought them. They were simple. They mentioned going to the Apple store to check out the iPhone since they hadn't yet seen one in person. At the time, I'd only known one person who owned the phone. He was a year older than me. A senior in my geometry class who I later found out was a weed dealer. And he kept it out on his desk for the first few weeks of the school year to show it off. It was the newest thing at the time, and we would all marvel at its sleek design and massive touch screen.

"Hey Étienne. Isn't that your friend?" Callum whispered, nudging my chin toward the first-floor Starbucks entrance. Yes, this mall had more than one Starbucks.

It was Thad. He was walking with a group of his friends. They were headed south and about to turn left, heading east. Which is where we were going. *How did I not see you?* I looked around, pulse pounding. The timing could not have been better, or worse. Our two groups were walking at such a pace that we would have collided if none of us were looking. Thad had his head down. One of his friends gave me a look, realizing that he recognized me from somewhere. We most likely had a class or two together over the years. His other friend was definitely gawking at me. Heather, the one with the laugh.

Why wasn't he looking at me though? He had to have seen my brothers and me. And of all places for the two of us to run into each other, this was not it. I was with my family, and he was with his friends. We were too exposed. This was too public of a place for us to interact in.

We got close enough for me to hear their voices. And as we were about to converge with them, I began to smile and decided to add a friendly wave. Like the idiot that I am. None of them acknowledged it, not even Thad. They didn't even look in my direction, save Heather who continued to stare me down.

The group passed us as if we'd somehow disappeared from their vision. I held my breath. How could Thad so easily and so bluntly disregard me like that? He didn't even look in my direction. What was going on in his head? This wasn't the person I had gotten to know. The little warmth I possessed began to leave my body as my eyes started to swell and my chest became heavy.

"That was rude," growled Callum. He said it loud enough that it would have been impossible for Thad not to hear.

"Let's go." I grabbed both of my brothers, trying to hold in my irritation.

The boys ran into the Apple store to look at the iPods and gape at their futuristic new phone. They'd been asking my mom to get them an iPod like mine, but she thought they'd ruin it before its first charge. I decided to sit on the bench outside the store and fiddle with the pivoting screen of my Sidekick. My nerves and negative thoughts reappeared. Was this it? Had he decided to move on and forget about me? Had he picked a side?

Callum tapped my shoulder a few minutes later. "Hey. Come on, Étienne."

"What? You guys just went in."

"We looked at stuff and that was it," Niall said.

"Call Mom and tell her we're going to the food court. I want a slice of pizza," Callum demanded.

The mall was so big that it messed with the signal on everyone's cell phones, so I sent her a text to meet us in the food court near the elevators. The food court was on the top floor overlooking the entire atrium. I held on to Niall's hand as he dragged me through the crowd of people standing still and blocking the way up the three sets of escalators. Seriously though, if you're going to use an escalator and not walk, stand on one side for people to pass.

I held on to Niall's hand so I wouldn't run into people. My mind and eyes were preoccupied, examining every inch around me for a chance to see him again.

On the third floor, the twins made me save a table directly across from the Starbucks stand that overlooked the atrium while they used my mom's credit card to grab food. I sat there and looked up at the glass ceiling, supported by thousands of steel beams, and wondered how such a massive structure could exist. It really was an engineering feat, and a work of art.

"Hi." Someone slid into the banquette next to me, his shoulder resting against mine. It wasn't someone. I knew that soft, masculine voice. I pretended not to hear him and continued to gaze toward the ceiling. If I looked into his eyes, I think I would have broken down.

"Please, Étienne. I'm a piece of shit. I... I didn't know what to do down there." His voice cracked; the vibration of his shaking body transferring to me as he leaned in. He too was about to fall apart.

My eyes met with his as they began to swell. I tried to push down the frog in my throat. I didn't need to say anything, he knew how much that hurt. I bit my lip, eyes wide, and sat up as I remembered the letter in my wallet. I reached around and pulled the wallet out of my back-left pocket. If I wanted to say something to him, the letter was the only thing that would suffice. So

I pulled it out and handed it to him, trying to force a small grin. He tried to open it, but I placed my hand on his and whispered, "Not here. Later." I reached my other hand under the table to briefly and discretely lace my fingers with his before he had to leave.

"I just... I can't lose him," I said to myself, alone at the table as his figure gradually faded from sight.

FRIDAY 20 JUNE 2008

24

BROTHERS

"What do I want to do today?" I asked myself after learning that I didn't have to work. Jason called me early in the morning and said I didn't need to come in. I was happy, but also annoyed that my next check would be smaller with this day off. But hey, I would only be seventeen once. My life could wait a moment before being required to devote every waking minute to a job I would end up hating, consuming my life and influencing my every decision.

"You're off?" My mom peeked her head into the doorway.

"I guess. Why?"

What does she want me to do now?

"I'm dropping the boys off at the public pool for swim lessons. Can you go with them and walk them home after, so I don't have to leave work?" she begged.

What else did I have to do? Mope about waiting for Thad. No, I needed to find a distraction if I wasn't going to work. So I agreed, then grabbed my swim bag and packed my stuff. They would be doing swim lessons for at least an hour, leaving me to sit there on the deck bored out of my mind. Or think about Thad. Or worry about seeing someone from school. I would hang out on the other side of the pool and go for a swim to distract myself.

"Give me your bags. I'm going to be over there on the other side. Come to me when you're done," I said once we exited the locker rooms.

It was still too early for the pool to be crowded, which was perfect for me. The less people I had to see from school the better. It's not that I hated everyone, I just didn't enjoy the company of most people. I was that person who hung out with the house pet whenever I was invited over. Also, there was less of a chance to run into someone who may have heard about Thad and me. If Dana did, there were bound to be more.

The sun wasn't quite high enough yet to get a good tan, though it was unusually hot for an early morning. I walked to the other side of the deck and claimed a pool chair beside the tall, white brick wall that bordered the back of the pool area, dividing the pool from the city library parking lot. Just one chair for me; my brothers could fend for themselves if they wanted to stay after lessons. I wasn't going to be an inconsiderate hog. If there's one thing that aggravates me, it's seeing unused pool chairs claimed by someone sitting next to it. *"Oh, I'm saving it for someone. They're on the way,"* they always say. *"Yeah well, I'm here right now and need a chair,"* I'd want to reply.

"I guess I'll get in," I said in my normal voice as no one was around to hear me speaking to myself. I got up after waiting a few minutes to see if the sun beamed any stronger. It was still too early, so I picked the lane furthest from the students. I didn't want to run into anyone. Then I began swimming a 200-meter freestyle to get my body warmed up. The water was too warm for a swimmer's liking, which made me feel more winded than normal and caused me to gasp for air with every other stroke. I reached the 125-meter mark and had to stop to catch my breath. *Damn, I'm out of shape.* Track season had recently finished, but that's a different world from swimming. Swimming takes everything out of you, working muscles you didn't even know the human body possessed.

"Who the…" I looked to the side after a kickboard collided with my left shoulder.

"Étienne, come here." Niall signaled from a few lanes over.

Their instructor was motioning me to come and join the group of students, most of whom were under the age of ten, from what I could tell. I took a deep breath, dove to the pool floor, and let the backs of my hands scrape against the tile as I fluttered my feet. There really is nothing like being underwater.

"Yeah," I spat as my face broke the surface, hands involuntarily pulling my curly hair to the side.

"Étienne, could you swim down to the other end and swim back? Freestyle," asked Andrew, the swim instructor.

"Uh. Okay. How slow? Do you want me to exaggerate the motions?"

Andrew was the swim team captain when I was a freshman. I didn't think he would remember my name after not seeing me for over two years. Well, I assumed most people didn't know my name. Not that it mattered. Andrew was a different kind of guy. Even different from Thad. He was kind to everyone from the get-go, including me. And he was friends with everyone. We later went to the same university, though he was in grad school by the time I started my undergrad. We'd run into each other around campus, and he'd always try to say hi. He made it a point to say hello to someone he knew, no matter how inconvenient or awkward. Unlike me. I tried my hardest to not get people's attention, and still do. Yes, I saw you. No matter what I said, I knew you were there. I still chose to remain unseen.

Andrew wanted me to swim back and forth, alternating between strokes, while the students dunked underwater to watch my movements. Then he explained the positions of my arms, legs, and my head afterward. I was never the fastest swimmer—that didn't matter to me. What mattered was my form. My swim coach used to film me swimming and used the videos to educate her younger swim students. Well, that's what she would tell me. My body drifted across the surface of the water with grace, and I loved it.

Winning isn't always winning. Remember that.

"Thanks, Étienne." Andrew reached his hand out to shake mine.

Why are you so nice?

"No problem. You don't have to go easy on my brothers. They're more capable than they look," I joked.

The sun was finally high enough by the time I got out, so I decided to lie on the pool chair, facing east while the kids practiced what Andrew and I taught them. I pulled my iPod out of the side pocket of my swim bag and put my new playlist on shuffle; the first song of which was "Sunrise Projector" by Tycho. It was the perfect music to lose myself to and drift away as the rays of the sun warmed my Mediterranean skin.

I closed my eyes for a while and let my thoughts dissolve into nothingness. Finally, a moment so peaceful I'd forgotten who I was. But only for a moment.

I was studying the little white flecks in my vision when a shadow stepped in front of the bright orange that lit up the inside of my eyelids. I cracked my eyes open and squinted, thinking it was someone unintentionally in front of me waiting for a friend. My heart sank, forcing my eyes wide open. They were not ready for the unfiltered sunlight as she stepped to the side, nearly blinding me. It felt like I was in a nightmare. I immediately pulled my shirt from behind me and tried covering myself. I needed to dissolve back into the chair where she couldn't see me.

"So. You and Thad. I don't think so," she said, standing in my way. Hands on her hips.

Heather. She was probably the shortest of Thad's friends— but never let someone's size define their intent or strength.

Heather was the powerhouse of the girls' soccer team. She was known by everyone, but only reachable by few. Thad being one of them. He'd never spoken about his friends when we were together, but I knew who she was.

"Um. Hi," I squeaked. She was more intimidating than she looked. Her condescending tone dragged out any ounce of self-worth left inside of you. "What was that?" I added, pretending I didn't hear her.

"You heard what I said. It's not happening," she sneered then sashayed away.

Not happening? Who is she? The calm that inhabited my body moments earlier evaporated through my skin within an instant. The morning swim fortified my happiness for the day, then it was peeled away from me as easy as washing off a newly pressed temporary tattoo. I should not have gone there that morning. I was too exposed.

"You alright?" asked Callum as the twins approached.

The two of them grabbed their bags from next to my chair. They were finished with their lessons. I had already gone to the locker rooms and re-clothed myself. I needed to cover as much of my body as possible. This was no longer a safe environment for me to be in.

"Fine," I said. "Let's go."

"Can we get a snow cone on the way out?" asked Niall.

I wanted to say no. Being there even a few minutes longer would have made my stomach turn over. But I said yes. They wanted snow cones from the concession stand, and if that was what it took to keep them calm and quiet during the walk home, then so be it.

Why was I so scared back there? I didn't understand. I shouldn't have cared what Heather thought of me. *Who is she anyway?* She was one of Thad's closest friends. That's who she was. She could get into his head. He was already second guessing himself. How was I going to compete with someone like that?

Maybe she was being protective of her friend. The way Dana was being with me.

Does she not like that Thad might like guys? That couldn't be it, though. She had an older brother who was gay. He was a senior when we were freshmen. The two of them clung to each other that entire year. What could it have been, then? I wasn't that ugly, was I? Was it the Coke-bottle glasses I wore sometimes when my contact lenses were bothersome?

"Do you want to go for a walk later with Frankie?" asked Niall. He hadn't finished his snow cone in time, and it was dripping down his arm.

Nasty, I thought. Anything sticky makes me squirm.

"We can do that. But after I shower. You guys need to shower too," I said. We had just been swimming, which in their eyes meant we were clean. We were not.

"So. What happened to your friend Étienne?" Callum looked over at me as we waited for the crosswalk light, cars slowing down as they passed by the police station across from the library.

"Yeah, what's his name? Thad. That was rude at the mall," Niall added.

He had a point. It was rude. But I forgave him. And why were they asking me this? I was not ready to be talking about my first romance with my little brothers.

"Yeah it was," I said. "But it's okay. It happens."

"You know we know he's more than a friend, Étienne," said Callum, the ticking of the crosswalk light counting down in the distance.

I kept straight, trying to ignore what my little brother said. We were only a few blocks from home. *When is this going to end?*

Callum caught my eye again. "You know we don't care, Étienne. We're not like dad."

"That's not fair, Callum. He's—"

Callum stuck his hand in the air, cutting me off. "What? He was mean to you."

Niall nodded in agreement.

I knew Callum was more observant than Niall. Niall was the silly, oblivious one of the two. They really did fill in where the other lacked. I didn't know, though, how much they had noticed. After they were born, and as I became older, my dad treated the two of them like his best buds. I didn't think they even noticed me. I was the distant older brother who didn't like to have fun. Their idea of fun. Maybe there was more to them than I thought. I guess I wasn't giving them enough credit.

The twins ran into the only two showers that we had in the house before I could grab a change of clothes, which left me with having to take a cool shower after they were done. I didn't mind though; cool water is better for the skin anyway. We took Frankie as planned and walked to one of the elementary school playgrounds close by. The two of them competed to see who was able to jump the furthest off the swings while Frankie was on the grass, spread eagle. It wasn't what I would have chosen to do with my day, but it was a good distraction. It kept my mind from thinking of the horrible things Heather could be saying to the only person in the world I really liked.

Hey. Thad texted me as I unhooked the leash from Frankie's collar. We had returned from our long walk. I refilled Frankie's water bowl with ice water and ran to my room to reply to the message. My heart was pounding, mind was racing. This was it. He was finally ready to talk to me.

Heyy, I replied.

Can I call you? he asked.

Of course. You of all people can.

There was an awkward silence when I first answered. We were both nervous. He was probably still unsure of how he wanted to be with me. While I was terrified that he was calling to end everything.

I broke the ice. What did I have to lose? Everything. "I hung out with my twin brothers today. Imagine how that was?"

"You rolling your eyes. That's what I imagine."

I recounted my day at the pool with the boys and how I was able to show off my swimming skills and then relax in the sun. I left out the part about his friend Heather. Our conversation needed to be positive. And I didn't want that interaction to discourage him.

"I wish I could have come," he finally said.

You wish you could have been with me? That's a good start.

"I had practice today with my hockey club. But I didn't go to skating lessons."

"Why not? Do you not like it anymore?" I asked, knowing he wouldn't quit skating lessons unless he had to.

"No, I do. I actually really like it. My dad won't pay for lessons anymore."

"Why not?" I bit my lip. I knew why.

"I guess it's punishment."

"That's not fair. It helps you with hockey, doesn't it?"

"It sucks. But whatever," he said, then sighed before perking up and adding, "My parents aren't going to be home tomorrow night. Want to hang here?"

Yes. You don't even have to ask.

His parents planned on going to a baseball game that night and decided to get a hotel room at one of the casinos in downtown Detroit, leaving the house to him and his sister. He mentioned, though, that his sister wasn't going to be home either, not that I think she would have cared. I didn't know her, but I'd hoped she wasn't as uptight as their parents.

"That'd be cool," I responded.

"I'm sorry about the other day. That wasn't fair." He lowered his voice.

"It's totally fine. I can't be mad. Who knows what I would have done if it were reversed?"

Actually, I did. I would have spotted him from a mile away and hid. It was being with my brothers that distracted me from seeing him, forcing me to continue my forward motion that day in the mall.

"I was thinking of maybe inviting two or three people." He gulped loud enough for me to hear it through the phone.

"Are you sure? You don't have to do that if you're not ready."

He hadn't even met my friends yet, though I was unsure if I still had any. Kayla and Samantha weren't mad at me. At least I didn't think they were. I hadn't heard from anyone after Dana's party.

"I like you, Étienne. I think as much as you like me. Maybe it'll work out."

SATURDAY 21 JUNE 2008

25

I ASKED THE MOON

I woke Saturday morning with butterflies in my stomach. I was finally going to see the inside of Thad's house, and maybe his room. He had been in mine. He knew some of the most intimate parts of my life and now it was my turn to know his. We had planned for me to arrive before anyone else so we could spend some time alone together. Then he'd introduce me to the friends he felt comfortable telling. Against my advice, he didn't want to tell them in advance. I would have at least warned them that a new friend would be there, but that's me.

"You look bright eyed," said Riley as I repositioned my glasses. I was in the bathroom getting ready for the day and tried putting in my contacts, but my eyes were too dry. I would try to put them in again later before going to Thad's.

"Uh. Thanks. What are you doing today?" I tapped the back of her shoulder before she could walk away.

"I'm leaving in a bit. Going to the pool with Nate, Alyssa, and Ashley."

"Oh. Okay. Do you think you could remember to feed Frankie tonight? I won't be home to feed him."

"Ooh. Going out." She winked. "Yeah, whatever."

My sister had become less snippy with me since our talk in the laundry room. I also thought things between her and my mom and grandma were cooling down. She was normally a pleasant person, but she was also the kind of person who feasted on negativity when it presented itself.

The rest of my day was altogether boring. I didn't have to work until later the next day. My mom decided to take on a few new patients, leaving me at home with the boys again while she made house visits. They spent most of their morning playing on the Wii. Then we took Frankie for a walk to the ice cream shop. We didn't need to. We'd already gone a few times during the week. But it was summer. They were kids. And my brothers were starting to grow on me.

My parents are leaving soon. Come over around eight, Thad texted.

I couldn't wait for eight o'clock that night. I put together the perfect outfit and even re-ironed everything to make sure I looked clean and crisp. My hair lay perfectly over the side of my face, and the curls were loose enough thanks to the low humidity that day. I tried to put my contact lenses in again, but even after rubbing them clean in my palms with solution, they still flipped around and blurred my vision.

People with astigmatism don't have perfectly curved corneas like the rest of the world, in case you didn't know. Ours are crooked. When we want to wear contacts, we need the ones with tiny weights in them to hold the lenses correctly in place. If it moves while it's in your eye, it's a headache trying to get it back into the right position.

"Argh," I grunted, then threw the contacts back into their case and grabbed my glasses.

Really? Today of all days I have to wear these ridiculous things. Standing in the mirror, I grimaced at my obstructed face. This was not what I had planned. Thad had never seen me with glasses. Not even the night he stayed over—I pushed through the discomfort and slept with the contact lenses in. Trust me, if you saw what I saw in the mirror you'd agree that spectacle-less Étienne was the better choice. Contact lens Étienne was the fashionable boy who didn't have to constantly touch his face to reposition the glasses slipping from his nose.

When I arrived at his house, I stood on the porch for a minute holding my glasses up against the porch light to make sure there weren't any smudges. A car passed by unusually slow, but the tinted windows blocked my efforts to see who was inside.

"I didn't know you wore glasses." He laughed as he opened the door.

I grunted. "My contacts were being stupid. I look like an idiot."

"I think they're cute. Come in." He stepped to the side then grabbed my hand as he closed the door.

So, this is it. His two-floor house was larger than my family's ranch style. It's not that it was much larger. It seemed grander thanks to its open floor plan. The entrance led to a two-story foyer, exposing parts of the second floor. Then the open living room to the right flowed without any obstruction into the kitchen toward the back of the house, which had a large opening to the left that connected to the dining room. Most of the rooms in my house were separated by thick walls, doorways, and even the kitchen was elevated by a few steps. Mine must have been built long before the conception of open floor plans.

He held on to my hand as he guided me through the house to grab a drink in the kitchen. He poured us both something from his dad's liquor cabinet. Then he took me up to his room.

"See. This is how a room should look," I said.

"What do you mean?" He shook his head, looking around.

"Well. Just look how ugly the wallpaper and carpet are in my bedroom."

His room was painted a calm light gray color and his floors

were wood. It's so much easier to clean wood than carpet. Especially when you have a dog and two little brothers running willy-nilly.

"You're crazy." He turned to face me, then nudged my chin upward and his eyes met mine.

He placed his hands on my hips, sending shivers up my spine. Then he moved in closer to kiss me.

"Shit." I pulled away; my vision distorted. "I hate these things."

I'd forgotten about my glasses, which his nose smudged. Another reason why I didn't usually wear the godforsaken things —I hate smudges. I'll never understand how people go about their day with gunk blocking their vision.

"I think you look smart with them on," he whispered. Then kissed me.

Do I look stupid without them? I opened my eyes and looked down at our locked lips. He was perfect. The kiss was perfect. I could finally let go of the fear that he didn't want me, because he did.

My eyes closed again so I could savor the short time we would have alone together. He put his arm around my body again and guided me to his bed. I lay back as he pushed his face further into mine and positioned his body over me. Our legs gradually intertwined as he combed my hair with his fingers. I pulled my right arm from his back and began to reach under his shirt, far enough to feel under the waistband of his jeans.

"Oh." He pulled away.

Damn. What's wrong with you, Étienne?

"I'm sorry. I shouldn't have done that." I pulled myself up and looked down in embarrassment. The moment was ruined. Why did I do that? He was not ready to go that far yet. *Why do you have to ruin everything, Étienne?*

"No. It's ahh. It's okay. I wasn't expecting it." He grinned nervously.

It was nearing the time his friends were supposed to arrive anyway, so the two of us descended to the kitchen to grab another drink. Thad sat on the sofa facing the large flat screen in the living room and set his drink on the coffee table. I stood near the entrance of the room, examining the large stereo.

"Ooh, it has an aux cable."

"Want to listen to some music?" He pointed to my front right pocket.

You know where I keep my stuff now, eh?

He encouraged me to connect the iPod so we could continue the playlist I had put together. We put on the stereo loud enough to enjoy the music, but not so much that we wouldn't hear a car pull up. I sat next to him, and we took a large sip of our drinks. He scooched closer to me, wrapped his left arm around my shoulder, and looked directly into my eyes. *This is all we need.* The two of us worked together. All we needed was some time alone to figure that out. Despite his problems, and mine, the world felt like it stopped when we were together. Nothing else mattered.

It's after nine now. Where are they? I wondered. His friends should have been arriving.

"What is this?" he asked, pointing toward the stereo. The playlist had come up to a song in French.

"This is Indochine. My favorite French band." I looked at the stereo.

"You know French?" He raised his brow.

"Yes and no." I grinned.

"How?"

"Well. My dad's mom was raised in French schools before Lebanon's independence from France. She used to sing to me in French as a child."

I understood it more than I admitted but didn't speak it much. Just like Arabic, I knew how to navigate French but feared sounding like an idiot if I tried speaking it. My second year at Wayne State University changed that. I enrolled in French courses and decided to push past my fear and relearn everything my grandma had taught me.

"What is he saying?" He tilted his head to the side. He was more interested than I thought he would be.

"The song is called, 'J'ai demandé à la lune.' I asked the moon, in English."

"Asked the moon what?" He winked.

An exact translation wouldn't have made much sense in English, so I tried thinking of how the song made me feel instead. "Bear with me." I exhaled. "So, he's asking the moon for advice, after being hurt by the sun. But she's not interested in helping. He then asks her if the sun still wants to be with him. But she laughs at him in the end."

It's more meaningful if you actually know French. I didn't think my summarization was the best, but I tried to show him how the song made me feel. How throughout my life, I tried showing people who I was. But the world hadn't made me feel like I was actually there, or that I was wanted. Like the singer, whenever I asked the moon for help, she chose not to.

"I like that." He looked down at the time on his phone screen before adding, "it's late. People are supposed to be here by now." He then pulled me closer.

He was right. Where was everyone? I didn't know who he had invited, but it had to have been at least two other people. He had more friends than I ever managed to have. *Could Heather have said something?* I scratched my head. She was peeved to see me at the city pool.

"Ope. Maybe that's them." He reached down to grab his dinging phone.

I took a peek at the message. *Sorry man, can't come. Something came up.*

He squeezed the phone and exhaled as he shrugged. It was nothing. He wasn't that bothered. Things happen. Right?

"What?" he said as another message appeared before he could put down the phone. The message read, *Hey man. I don't think we can come. Something came up.*

His face turned yellow as he took a gulp of his drink. He didn't tell me how many people he had invited, but it was apparent that none of them were coming. Thad was the cool guy with all the right friends. Why would they bail on him like that?

"They're not coming." He pulled his arm out from around me, resting his forearms on his knees.

"Did they know I'm here?" I asked.

"Kind of. I tried to explain it to them but left out some details about us." He looked at the door, probably hoping someone would knock.

"I'm sorry." I grabbed hold of his arm.

"Fuck them."

Yeah. What kind of friends are those?

He unlatched my hand from his arm, grabbed our empty glasses, then turned up the stereo. My eyes followed him until he turned the corner in the kitchen and headed toward the dining room where the sound of him fiddling through bottles in one of the cabinets overshadowed the music for a moment. He reappeared seconds later with a bottle of whisky in hand. Then collapsed into the sofa, colliding with my side. He took a swig straight from the bottle before handing it to me.

I don't know if I can do this. I looked down as the bottle opening touched my bottom lip. He put his hand on my thigh when the liquid made contact with my tongue, sending goose bumps throughout my body. I swallowed, then leaned back and closed my eyes to let whisky burn down my throat. Thad leaned over, grabbing onto me, and then locked his lips with mine. This was it. This was what we were both looking for. Not a soul in sight could scare us or stop us from being together. We belonged together, and he finally knew it.

I put my arms around him, pulling his body closer as I used

my legs to push myself up. He repositioned himself, legs strad-dling my waist as his phone vibrated. But he didn't answer. Being with me, being *on* me was more important.

"What the..." A deep voice drowned out the stereo.

Thad soared into the air, revealing both of his parents standing in the foyer. My stomach ascended into my throat. This man was much larger and obviously stronger than his son. Thad raised his hands to try to explain but his dad advanced, slapping his son across the face so hard that Thad dropped to the floor. I jumped out of the couch and raced to Thad's motionless body. Thad's mom screamed and tried to stop her husband as he directed his gaze toward me. He reached down, grabbed me by the back of my shirt and jeans, forcing my arms to unlock from Thad's immobile body.

What? Where? My eyes opened as I frantically searched for my glasses. My forehead was pulsating, and I felt a warm liquid running down my face. I squinted to try to sharpen my vision as I searched for my glasses but only felt the corner where two walls met. This must have been where I landed.

"Look what you did. You could be arrested. He's only a kid," his mom screamed from across the room.

I heard Thad sobbing as he called out my name. *Please come help me, Thad. I can't see anything. I can't feel anything.*

I finally found my glasses on the floor by my right hip. One of the temples had broken off while the other was severely bent. I pulled them in front of my face; one of the lenses was cracked in half. After trying to straighten the remaining temple, I tight-ened the pads to squeeze my nose so they wouldn't fall off, then tried to pull myself off the floor.

"Get out!" his dad bellowed.

"Dad, please," Thad blubbered as his mom held him back. Tears ran down the red mark appearing on the side of his face.

"Get out now." His dad pointed toward the door after I

finally pulled myself up and leaned against the wall, exhaling heavily.

"No. Étienne," cried Thad, his mom still holding him back.

"Shut your mouth," his dad said. "He's out of here. Or you are."

My eyes began to swell, and my throat grew sore as I watched my first love weeping on the other side of the room. He wanted me. He wanted to help me. But he was terrified of the giant standing between us. How was this the nice man who offered to help my mom all those years ago?

I stood motionless against the wall, amazed at the pain running through my body. I'd never in my life been physically abused like this. Never once been in a fight. The pain inside of me wanted to make itself heard. I wanted to scream.

"Dad stop. No," Thad yelled as his dad took another step toward me. "Please no. Étienne, go. Go. I'm sorry, Étienne. I'm so sorry."

There wasn't enough force in my body to move. Despite his son's incessant howling, Thad's dad grabbed me with one hand as he opened the front door with the other. Then he shoved me onto the steps of the front porch before slamming the door. I could hear the screams of two people inside as my right shoulder collided with the corner of the bottom step. I was sobbing—not just from the physical pain throbbing in my head and my shoulder, but from the pain of being separated from the only person who made me feel like I was allowed to be me.

I lost him.

SUNDAY 22 JUNE 2008

26

———

THANK YOU, RILEY

This isn't real. I tried opening my left eye, then my right. The sky was blue as far as I could see, except for the faint white of the moon still hanging in the morning sky. My glasses were still attached to my nose, though the massive crack and dried blood distorted my vision. My back was awkwardly curved, and my right shoulder throbbed when I tried to move. I was in my sister's hammock.

It's surprising my body even made it there the night before without collapsing. After spending a few minutes crawling down the steps of Thad's front porch, I used the railing to pull myself upright, then took one step at a time until I was confident enough not to fall. I reached the corner of his street and realized that the pain in my head, shoulder, and back wouldn't let up. My knees started to buckle. So I walked the next few blocks to my house as fast as my body would let me. I collapsed into the hammock, using the last remaining energy to adjust to a somewhat comfortable position.

Being in my own bed would have been better for my back. And a warm shower would have eased the beating in my head. But I couldn't go in. I couldn't chance my family seeing the dried blood splashed across my face, broken glasses clinging to my nose. My mom would have freaked out. She probably would have even called the police. No. I didn't want that. I wanted to be left in peace.

"Étienne. Oh my god. Oh my god, Étienne." My sister's long hair tickled my face as she peeked into the hammock.

Shit. No. I sat up, nearly head-butting her, and tried to shimmy my way out of the hammock. But I was too weak. My sister grabbed my left arm and wrapped it around her. "How'd you know I was here?"

"The twins came out a little while ago with Frankie and saw you. They came running to me. Come on, quick. Mom's in the shower." She lifted me out, then pulled me toward the back door.

"She can't know," I whispered.

"Étienne, what happened? Was it Thad? Did he do this?"

"No. It was someone else. I don't want to talk about it."

No way was I going to talk about it. Just thinking about the night before made my eyes water. Plus, what good would it have done? If I said something, someone else would have found out. Then my mom would find out. Then the police would be called. Then our neighbors would find out. I didn't want to put that on Thad. Imagine living with a dad like that.

"Étienne. What happened?" Callum started.

"Go now. Take your brother and hold the bathroom door shut to distract Mom. Don't say a word," said Riley, cutting him off.

She dragged me in over the doorstep then up the stairs to the kitchen and through the front sitting room. My mom was banging on the bathroom door while my brothers pulled as hard as they could on the handle and giggled loudly so she wouldn't hear Riley and I passing by. Luckily, my door was still shut from when I left. Riley cracked it open to let me in, then shut it quickly as I tried crawling into bed. I burrowed under the blankets and hid my face in between the pillows. My shoes were still attached to my feet, but I didn't care. I begged for the pain to stop, but it was too deep to be reversed.

"Hey," Riley whispered into my ear later on.

I couldn't fall asleep. I didn't want to fall asleep. I was afraid my mom would try to wake me and see my face. The bedroom door did creak open once before Riley came in. It was probably my mom. Thankfully my entire body was covered.

"What time is it?" I asked Riley. "Ugh, I have to go to work."

"No. You don't. I took your phone and told Rhonda you were really sick."

"What? When? I don't remember you coming in. Riley, I can't miss work," I protested.

"Have you looked in the mirror?"

No, I hadn't. I was afraid of what I would see. Nothing had ever happened to my face before, save a zit from time to time. But sitting there in bed, I could only imagine what it looked like, the dried blood on my skin cracking as I squinted.

"Go take a shower and meet me back in here. Hurry. Mom's with Grandma in the back room."

I did as I was told. I undressed and hid my bloody polo under the mattress in case my mom came snooping, then threw my jeans into the hamper. There was a scrape on the left knee of the jeans which I didn't care about; ripped jeans were still in style. In the bathroom I tried to avoid the mirror until after washing everything off. I took the hottest shower my skin could bare and used nearly half my bottle of cleanser to make sure nothing was left on my face. Then I stood under the shower head to try to ease the pain. After the shower I put in my contact lenses to see clearly for the first time in hours.

How am I going to explain that I need new glasses? I stared in the mirror. I hated glasses, but still needed them at night before going to bed, and in the morning.

I sighed as I looked in the mirror. Purplish blue marks

covered my left knee and right shoulder, along with a red scrape on my forehead. Fortunately, the bloody gash was mostly above my hairline, hidden under my curls. I would need to go to the store and try to find a concealer to cover up parts of my forehead and my right cheek. *Maybe Riley has something.*

With the towel wrapped around my body, I ran to my room and threw on a pair of jeans to cover my bruised knee. All my shirts covered my shoulders so there was no worry there.

Riley knocked at the door. "Can I come in?"

"Yeah," I whispered.

She opened the door, holding her makeup bag. I sighed, relieved. *You read my mind.*

She placed her makeup bag on my bed. Riley and I were the only ones left in the family with the darker complexion, so her shade of makeup would match my skin. Well, almost. Riley's skin was a little browner than my olive skin, but not by much. She had me sit on the edge of the bed and told me to close my eyes so she could cover up the red spots on my face.

"Ahh." I winced when she started to dab my forehead. It was more sensitive than I had anticipated.

"There," she said before handing me a small mirror from her bag.

It looked perfect. Nearly perfect. Like I went out in the sun and forgot to rub the sunscreen on all of my face. But it was good enough that my mom probably wouldn't notice. Riley let me have a few of her products and gave me a quick tutorial on how to use them properly.

"Thanks Riley."

"I still think you should say something. You look like shit. That's not cool."

Guess I look like shit. What are sisters for?

I decided I'd stay in my room for the rest of the day. My head continued to pulsate. And I didn't want to give my mom the chance to study my face. She would be the one to question the uneven tan. It was safer in my room.

I grabbed my notebook and a pen, skootched myself up the bed and rested my head on the pillows, then reached into my bedside table to grab my iPod from the drawer. Loud sounds probably would have bothered my injured head, but I didn't care. I needed my music. The ambient and trancey beats were the only thing that would put me at ease, besides Frankie.

"What?" I anxiously dissected the drawer. The iPod wasn't there.

No. No. No. It's at his house.

27

———

THE REUNION

Where am I?

I look around the room and realized I zoned out. Every face is pointed in my direction—blind stares and open jaws. Some with tears in their eyes. What happened? What's going on? A voice continues to talk at the head of the room near the entrance.

"My dad shoved him into a wall and knocked him out. And I did nothing. I did nothing to protect him, out of fear that some of you didn't want to be friends with *us*." He points to the table where his old friends sit. Heather is eying me. But this time her look is much softer.

Oh my. That's where I am.

Thad is standing at the podium in front of the mic, his swollen blue eyes emitting a few tears. "I'm sorry Étienne," he calmly says from above the mic.

I know why he was apologizing. It's not for what his dad did to me. He's apologizing for his behavior all those years ago. He regrets that he never responded when I reached out to him. I did, the night after. And even the day after that. I called him. I wanted to assure him that I was okay and that I still wanted to be

258

with him. But he never answered. He wouldn't even look in my direction when senior year started.

I felt nothing that year. I dropped out of my sports teams. My grades fell. All of my anxieties and insecurities returned as I pushed myself further into seclusion. I needed him the most during that time, and I'd hoped he needed me. But his life looked like it went back to normal. I envied that.

I look to the left of me. I'm still standing at the bar, drink in hand. Somehow it hasn't fallen. Dana is standing by my side. I have no idea when she arrived, but I'm happy to see her there, and immediately notice her blond hair, its natural color for the first time since we were kids.

I knew you wouldn't ditch me.

"I'm glad I got here in time." She smiles then hugs me as my eyes start to swell.

I look up from behind Dana as her arms are wrapped around me. Thad left the podium and is heading toward the two of us. My heart thumps—I'm not prepared to talk to him. We haven't spoken since that last night at his house eleven years ago. It began so wonderfully, then ended so violently. I really missed him. It's not often in life you're able to meet your other half at such an early age. He was my perfect match. I've compared him to everyone over the years, even when I was trying not to.

I let go of Dana as he comes closer.

He reaches into his front right pocket. "I have something for you," he says, then pulls out a small, weathered iPod.

"You kept it?" I look up at his teary face, my gaze meeting his. Time has been kind to him—his icy blue eyes and silvery blond hair are virtually unchanged.

"This little thing still works. I even listen to your playlist sometimes. Well, all the time. Especially the last song."

I remember that song— "Ride (Tiësto Remix)" by Cary Brothers.

I never really did lose you, did I?

ACKNOWLEDGMENTS

I would like to thank my Dachshunds, who never leave my side, and who were the culprits of several typos on the first draft.

To my wonderful partner Fred, thank you for always encouraging me to do better, and for supporting every dream I've tried to chase.

To Patrick and Pierra, thank you for providing me with a lifetime of childhood memories, nourishing my creativity.

Most importantly, to *you*. Thank you for giving me the opportunity to create a place where we can belong.

ABOUT THE AUTHOR

First and foremost, Paul loves his dogs.

Spending most of his child-hood living between Detroit and the mountains of Lebanon, Paul created a home for himself with fiction. A place where he and his characters could step out of the shadow and belong.

Photo by Frederick Tech

Paul is a Detroit-based author, a bilingual specialist in the tech industry, and a graduate of Wayne State University where he specialized in Near Eastern studies and French literature.

When Paul isn't working, he loves spending time with his stubborn Dachshunds, inventing stories with main characters who are as brave as he wishes he could be, and listening to 2000s dance music.

twitter.com/itsPaulARayes

instagram.com/itspaularayes

tiktok.com/@itspaularayes

SUPPORTING INDIE AUTHORS

How to support independent authors:

Buy and read our books.

(This affords us the time and inspiration to continue writing.)

Give our books as gifts.

(Who doesn't love a new book?)

Engage with us on our digital platforms.

(As independent authors, our resources can be limited. This engagement is essential to getting our names out there and conquering the merciless algorithms.)

Request our books from your local library.

(This supports us without any out-of-pocket cost to the reader. It also creates author exposure in areas where we may be left out.)

Write reviews on retailer websites and Goodreads.

(This creates awareness and helps our books stand out in the market.)

~ Your support is appreciated ~

Thank you

www.ingramcontent.com/pod-product-compliance
Lightning Source LLC
Chambersburg PA
CBHW061234310726
48971CB00007B/2067